I0573413

PROJECT NEMESIS

THE LONG RUN: BOOK ONE

LEAH R CUTTER

KNOTTED ROAD PRESS

Project Nemesis
The Long Run: Book One
Copyright © 2022 Leah Cutter
All rights reserved
Published by Knotted Road Press
www.KnottedRoadPress.com

Cover Art:
Illustration 218640067 © Tiziano Cremonini | Dreamstime.com

ISBN: 978-1-64470-307-6

Cover and interior design copyright © 2022 Knotted Road Press
http://www.KnottedRoadPress.com

Reviews
It's true. Reviews help me sell more books. If you've enjoyed this story, please consider leaving a review of it on your favorite site.

Come someplace new...
Are you a traveler? Do you enjoy exploring strange new worlds, new cultures, new people?

Journey into the various lands envisioned by Leah Cutter.

Sign up for my newsletter and I'll start you on your travels with a free copy of my book, *The Island Sampler*.

http://www.LeahCutter.com/newsletter/

ALSO BY LEAH R CUTTER

Science Fiction

The Long Run

Project Nemesis

Project Nyx

Project Tisiphone

Project Persephone

War of the Allied Worlds

The Labors of Darius Linard

Huli Intergalactic: Science/Space Fantasy

Origins

The Strawberry Girl

Urban/Contemporary Fantasy Series

The Cassie Stories

Poisoned Pearls

Tainted Waters

Spoiled Harvest

Bloodied Ice

The Witch's Progress

Circle of Air

Circle of Fire

Epic Fantasy Series

Houses of the Dead

Houses Divided

Houses Fallen

Houses Reborn

Forgotten Gods

A Wind Blown Torment

A Stone Strewn Clash

A Sea Washed Victory

The Tanesh Empire Trilogy

The Glass Magician

The Desert Heart

The Ghost Dog

Mysteries

The Purloined Letter Opener

The Tell Tale Heart Pin

Dancer in Darkness

Trophy Hunters

The Alvin Goodfellow Case Files

The Rabbit Mysteries

The Shredded Veil Mysteries

Mystery, Crime, and Mayhem

INTRODUCTION

I've always referred to the first book in this series as *Leverage* meets *Star Trek*. Though, by the later books, I was referring to the series as *Leverage* versus The Evil *Star Trek* Federation.

Leverage holds a very special place in my heart. I mean, who doesn't love good competence porn? (And if you haven't seen the TV show *Leverage*, it's like the movie *Ocean's Eleven*, only done in a weekly format. Capers with a revenge theme.)

The writers on *Leverage* were awesome. John Rogers has a special place in my heart, to be honest. I was able to ask him once about whether or not the writers had ever heard of Lester Dent.

His response? The essay by Lester, which details how to write modern fiction, was printed out and hanging on the wall of the writing room. (Here's a link: http://www.paper-dragon.com/1939/dent.html)

I started this series with the concept of a five-man band. I did a lot of world building, figuring out what the equivalent of a phone would be, what the transportation mechanism was, as well as the aliens.

I also started by using Damon Suede's *Activate* method,

basically, coming up with a verb for each character, then using those as the inspiration for all their actions and interactions.

This has been a blast to write. My first readers have each had a favorite character, however, they'd all had a *different* favorite.

This is a good problem to have.

I hope that you also enjoy these books, this lighter take on crime and the future.

Enjoy!

Leah R Cutter
July 2022
Ravensdale, WA

CHAPTER 1

JUDIT

JUDIT KOVÁCS, Human captain and proud owner of the new-to-her spaceship *Ferdinand II*, turned into the hallway leading from her cabin to the front of the ship and banged her shoulder against the damned corner.

As usual.

"A fenébe!" she cursed in Hungarian as she hurried forward.

"Graceful as always?" Saxon, her second-in-command, asked from his seat as she came walking into the main helm, still rubbing her shoulder.

Judit thought about gracing him with a few choice Hungarian curses. However, just because they'd be in Hungarian didn't mean that Saxon wouldn't know or understand them. He'd heard enough of them while working with her over the past eight years.

Besides, then he might reply with some of his own, from his native Yu'udir, and then they'd be stuck cursing at each other for an hour or more, coming up with even more new and inventive phrases. Not that that happened frequently.

Usually, it only occurred when they were drunk. Or something like that.

Saxon may have sounded like a British university professor when he spoke Common, but he was covered in short white fur and stood over two meters tall. The skin of his face was pitch-black, with searing blue eyes that peered out intelligently. His hands had black palms and claws that he kept well-trimmed. That day, he wore a double-breasted, brown tweed vest, but no cap.

Instead of replying, Judit slid into the captain's chair and pointedly asked, "How close are we to the station?"

They'd just passed out of the hyperspace gate and into the Kembag system. While no one monitored the gates leaving the hyperspace tunnels, the gates entering hyperspace were all controlled by The Universal Trading Cartel.

Judit pushed her butt back further into the chair, trying to get the gel to activate and actually start cushioning her, damn it. She'd reprogramed the chair to respond to her weight and height at least three times now, but it stubbornly held onto the previous owner's preferences, which appeared to be with the seat ramrod straight and the cushions as hard as rocks.

"About three hours out, short run," Saxon replied.

Judit looked up, through the front windows of the spaceship. However, she couldn't make out the station in the distance. She ran her finger over a dial on the arm of her chair, bringing up a screen. It hovered above the console in front of the windows, a 2-D hologram, giving her a better view of what lay ahead.

The Kembag system was primarily settled by the Bantel. The uncharitable would call them chameleons, based on their similarity to the lizard that originally came from Earth. Just as they might call Saxon a Yeti. Though they were both bipedal, with symmetrical limbs. You didn't get into *different* until you started looking at the Khanvassa or the Oligochuno.

Space stations seemed to come in two designs: one or more discs rotating around a central core, or weirdly organic and distinctly asymmetrical, with the oldest parts of the station in the center and the newer pieces randomly attached later.

Thankfully, the Mawar station appeared to be the former and not the latter. While Judit sometimes enjoyed those older stations, getting lost while exploring them, but today was not the day for that sort of frivolity.

She had a schedule, and a pretty narrow window for delivering her cargo. If she made it early, she'd get a bonus. She checked the countdown clock, and she was not.

Maybe next time.

As it was, given a three-hour short run from the system gate into the station, she should be smack dab in the middle of her delivery window. No bonus, but no penalties either.

That is, if she didn't get shunted to some back lane when approaching the station.

She really didn't have the budget to pay a penalty. Not when *Ferdinand II* still needed so many upgrades. She glanced around the helm, noting what she'd like to change next.

The main helm was cramped, at least as far at Judit was concerned. Though it had been built for Humans, and she'd spent her entire life in ships or on stations, this particular helm made her claustrophobic at times. Maybe it was the way the ceiling sloped, making Judit always feel as though she stood in the center of a bubble, unable to straighten up around the edges. Or perhaps it was the awful color scheme—seriously, who painted all the walls in shades of orange, covered the floor in black rubber, and put red lights in every display? (It was part of what she hated so much about the captain's chair. That dirty brown-orange was *not* her color.)

Or maybe it was because the windows at the front of the helm were tiny compared to the rest of the space, sixty centimeters wide and only thirty tall. It wasn't as if they were a military ship and needed to put up blast shields to protect themselves. No, the former owners had just flown everywhere looking at screens and never at what they were actually flying toward. They relied on the ship's programming instead of their own instincts.

She understood the logic. Smaller windows made a ship seem "serious." Large windows were for cruise liners and tourists.

After she repainted and changed out all the display lights, she'd rip off the top of this ship. Install windows that took up the whole front end. She didn't care if it made the front of the ship look square and unsymmetrical. There was no reason for any spaceship to be streamlined, at least as far as she understood the physics of moving through space.

But that "someday" was pretty far off in the future. For now, she needed to deal with her current job.

She flipped a switch on the arm of her chair, opening up a channel to the second helm, where Brett, a Bantel, worked the communications for the ship. Another Human, Xidong, monitored the sensors from there, making sure debris didn't show up out of nowhere and smack into them.

"Brett, make sure you contact the station as soon as we get in range," Judit said.

"On it!" came Brett's obnoxiously cheery voice.

Judit couldn't help but shudder. How could a person always be so happy? But it was a general characteristic of all of the Bantel.

That, plus the fact that they could change their skin color to whatever they chose, including blending into whatever background they happened to be standing in front of if they stood completely still.

It was one of the reasons why the Bantel wore clothing that frequently had either patterns or colors that clashed. Or both. It was their way of getting you to trust them. They couldn't disappear in such outfits.

Judit only had a Bantel on her crew because Saxon had insisted on giving Brett a chance.

Stupid loyal Yu'udir and their stupid loyalty.

But Judit wouldn't trust one of the Bantel as far as she could throw one. And she could heave a member of the smaller race quite far. They generally stood no taller than one hundred and thirty-five centimeters, and tended to be quite slender and graceful.

Though Judit had a few extra pounds on her—on the squishy side as one of her ex's had referred to her— underneath those she was mostly muscle. Good peasant stock as her mother had joked. She wasn't as wide as a Khanvassa— a beetle like being who grew their own armor—but she wasn't thin and svelte like a damned worm either. She was in her mid-forties and deserved a few extra curves. And pounds.

"Anything out there we should avoid, Xidong?" Judit inquired, just to include him in the conversation.

After a few long seconds, Xidong finally replied. "Nothing for us to worry about."

"Sounds good," Judit said, faking her light tone.

She flipped the switch to close the channel with a defiant gesture. "Bah," she said.

Saxon merely nodded. They'd discussed the situation more than once.

This was the initial voyage of *Ferdinand II*, at least for Judit and this crew. She'd departed from her home space station of *Záhony* decades before, leaving behind her family and siblings. She'd started with one of the local traders,

Miklós, who'd treated her like a long-lost granddaughter, worked with him for years, scraping by and saving every credit she could. When he'd retired eight years before, she inherited his cargo ship, *Levente*.

Eventually, she'd managed to save enough to buy a newer ship, *Ferdinand II*. Saxon had been the only one who'd come with her from the old crew. Everyone else had retired when the ship had.

Judit couldn't afford a top-of-the-line ship. *Ferdinand II* had stretched her finances out as far as she could go and still not be in (too much) debt.

Of course, if she'd join The Universal Trading Cartel and stopped insisting on being an independent cargo carrier, she could have gotten a much larger and nicer ship, one that fit her like a glove.

However, then she'd be stuck in the Cartel for the rest of her life, making the same run over and over again until she keeled over. Just another cog in one great big stupid machine.

The reason Judit couldn't wait to leave *Záhony* was due to how tiny of a space station it was. Everyone knew everyone else. Everyone was always in everyone else's business. It was like growing up in the small Hungarian village of the same name back on Earth, with less than four thousand people.

No, Judit had wanted to see the universe, to travel to the exotic worlds she saw on the vids, to make friends with all the various species, including the elusive Chonchu. She wanted to have adventures everywhere she went.

Mostly, she'd succeeded, when she wasn't busting her ass over cargo, scraping and scrimping to get by.

Some members of the original crew of *Ferdinand II* had stayed with the ship. After this initial shake-down run, she would come to a decision about whom she would keep, like Sorrel who handled her cargo. He was an Oligochuno, and looked like a giant earthworm. He had a natural ability to rotate objects in three dimensions in his head to get everything to fit perfectly. And maybe she'd keep Xidong, though she'd have to have a talk about him actually doing his damned job and not playing those elaborate video games of his between scans.

But Brett was probably going to have to go. She'd been competent enough, but too damned cheery. Plus, she had a way of questioning everything that Judit asked her to do, being slyly subversive.

However, Judit didn't have to worry about any of that today.

Today, she was completing her first run. Going to get it into the station on time. Then go and celebrate while contemplating where she was going to find a new crew.

One thing at a time. One day at a time.

Or as her mother had always jokingly said, *Egyszerre egy kecske:* one goat at a time.

CHAPTER 2
ARTHUR

ARTHUR WAS ALWAYS surprised at how *long* his general briefing meetings were, the ones he held once a week on the first day of the week. He scratched at his white fur absent-mindedly, noting that his black claws needed to be trimmed soon. As soon as the one chap finished up, Arthur shifted in his chair and indicated for the next report to start. At least most of the heads of staff had already spoken and he only had two more to go.

It wasn't as if everyone kept the same standard eight day schedule that he as a Yu'udir kept on his space station *Camelot*. The Oligochuno worked four and two, the Khanvassa did ten and one, though they did have a number of holy days when they didn't work.

However, after two days off, it was as if the news from everywhere had piled up higher than a snowdrift in a windy valley.

The conference room he and the rest of his staff sat in was well appointed and not *generic*. That had been one of the many things Arthur found intolerable at the Cartel's headquarters. They could afford a little personality in their meeting rooms. Instead, they insisted that all the rooms look identical.

Today, Arthur and his heads of staff were meeting in the Round Table Room. There was also the Jungle Room, the Nebula Room, the Sun Room, the Mountain Room, and so on. Arthur had used a set designer instead of an interior decorator for all his high concept work. She had yet to disappoint him.

Of course, the primary feature of the Round Table Room was a huge round table. It wasn't carved out of actual wood. Though Arthur could have afforded it, he'd instead chosen the best simulation possible that looked like tough, scarred, heavy oak. Only an expert could tell the difference. Maple and mahogany inlays filled the center of the table, making it appear like a gigantic pie that had been sectioned into twenty-four slices. The chairs were all different as well, each suited for the race who sat on it. The sideboard looked as though it was a built-in wooden cabinet, with a leaded glass cupboard above. Snacks and various beverages filled it, as some of the races enjoyed constant nibbling.

"Then, there's the Kembag system," Fran brought up. He was the head of security for *Camelot*, Arthur's Lancelot, as it were. "It's a Bantel system," he added with a grin.

As Fran was himself a Bantel, Arthur merely nodded, unsure of which of the several regular behaviors the Bantel engaged in that Fran was referring to.

Fran wore his usual black-and-white checked shirt, this time matched with a pair of hot-pink trousers. He wasn't likely to disappear in that outfit anytime soon. His bulging eyes were bright green that morning. The rest of his visible, scaly skin was a pale yellow.

"Seems that they're running a scam. Again," Fran said, glancing down at his notes.

Arthur would have said, "As usual," but he didn't want to insult Fran. Not in front of the others, anyway.

It was fine to tease his head of security when they were in private. However, in public, Fran needed to be shown the utmost respect. The Bantel had kept Arthur alive since before they'd moved to *Camelot*, ensuring that the many threats against Arthur's life never succeeded.

In *Camelot*, they controlled access to the station with an iron claw. There were fewer attempts against Arthur now, even if that meant less privacy for everyone.

"Every system has a quota of new recruits that they must acquire for the Cartel," Fran said, explaining to the rest of the staff.

That brought grumbles from the others. Arthur as well, though he at least always tried to maintain a veneer of civility in front of people.

It was all well and good to be over two meters tall, covered in fur, with claws and talons, howling at everything. That behavior was likely to intimidate most of the other species. However, that wasn't about to get you very far, now was it? Fear only motivated people for so long.

Much better to be civil and get along with everyone.

At least until it was appropriate to unsheathe one's claws.

"The Kembag system appears to have doubled the number of recruits they're sending along," Fran continued. "And we all know that people don't volunteer for the Cartel in huge numbers. They must be doing something to get so many recruits."

"Do they get a bonus for doing that?" Fennel, the Oligochuno asked. Zie represented the merchants and traders on the space station. Like the rest of the Oligochuno, zie had a long, skinny, yellowish-white body with an orange sensor ring taking up the top third of zir "head." The ring contained the equivalent of eyes, ears, and nose. Fennel's mouth was

11

below that and visible most of the time. Fennel, like other aliens who regularly came into contact with Humans and Yu'udir, had learned how to smile. However, Fennel stubbornly refused to look symmetrical, and kept zir arms to a minimum, only growing one when needed. Today, zie had just a single tentacle-like arm growing out of the center of zir chest that zie used for bringing a cup of tea to zir mouth.

As mating season for the Oligochuno was still quite far off, Fennel was in a neutral, genderless state, and so preferred gender-neutral pronouns. Once mating season started, zie would choose a gender, based on preference as well as compatibility with the closest Oligochunos.

Fran both shrugged his shoulders as well as tilted his head from side to side. For the races who didn't really have shoulders, such as the Oligochuno, the tilting of the head was how they indicated they weren't certain about something.

"I'd have to read their specific contracts to know that," Fran said. "However, I know other systems that receive that sort of incentive."

Arthur nodded, understanding the subtle question that Fran was asking: Was it worth his time to break into the Kembag system and "liberate" their contract files?

"Let's assume that your supposition is correct," Arthur said. "Why is it important?" He didn't mean to sound so put out. However, Masala, Arthur's *Merlin*, as it were, had a discovery to show him that afternoon. Something about how the newest spaceships were tunneling into hyperspace.

But Arthur wouldn't allow himself to meet with Masala until after his regular meetings were done. It was a treat he reserved for himself, a reward for sitting and listening to his staff.

Fran looked Arthur directly in the eye. "It might be a good time and place to get recruits for our program," he said casually.

Arthur sighed. "I see," he said.

On the one hand, Fran was absolutely correct. Arthur needed recruits. Pilots and crews willing to risk their lives on the experimental spaceships he was building.

On the other hand, Arthur would much rather that people came to him voluntarily, rather than it be a choice between a rock and a hard place: choosing to work for the Cartel or possibly dying a horrible death.

He knew what he'd choose. He'd chosen it many times already for himself, to work for himself and face possible death rather than work for the Cartel. Though officially he was still a member of the board of the Cartel, his family didn't control enough shares for him to be a voting member.

Not as if a single vote could change that much. No, it was much better to change the Cartel by forcing new technology on them.

Hence, the new spaceships, codename *Project Nemesis*.

As well as the new space stations, that no one on this team knew about.

"Yes, you should see if you can get some new recruits there," Arthur said heavily.

He assured himself that he wasn't like the rest of the Cartel, that he wasn't throwing lives away carelessly. No, any pilot who came to him, regardless of the circumstances, would be well taken care of.

Or at least their families and beneficiaries would be, if the worst occurred.

CHAPTER 3

JUDIT

JUDIT COULD COUNT on the fingers of one hand the number of times she'd been directed to dock so close to the main hub of a space station. It meant that her cargo would be unloaded more quickly, shuttled off to her client's warehouse, accounted for, and then she would get paid.

It wasn't going to be fast enough for her to get a bonus. However, it would look good on her record. It might make it easier for her to get the next job, the one out of this station and onto the next.

Judit was aware that if she would just find a single run and stick to that, she wouldn't have to hustle so hard. However, she'd probably also have turned into a murderous psychopath after her third such run.

Ferdinand II was much larger than *Levente* had been. Much newer as well. Judit had taken three days practicing taking off and landing after she'd acquired it. While she could let the computer handle all of those maneuvers, what would happen when (not if) the computer navigation system died at some critical point?

No, it was much better for her to be able to fly the damned ship herself.

Some of the smaller stations, like *Záhony*, the one she'd grown up on, didn't have full landing pads. Instead, they had a large number of airlocks and connecting gangplanks.

Mawar, though, had full docks that you drove spacecraft into, straight into the station itself. Even larger transport ships like *Ferdinand II*.

Saxon sat silently beside her as she toggled levers and used the stick to land them precisely in the center of their assigned berth, landing pad number fourteen. They touched down with a slight bump, nothing jarring.

Next time, she'd make sure to just kiss the platform, landing so smoothly that no one would feel it.

"Nice job, my dear," Saxon said, beaming at her.

"Thanks," Judit said. She blew out a long breath and flexed her fingers. She'd been more tense landing than she normally was. Then again, this was a new ship, in a new place.

She toggled the switch on the comm to speak with Sorrel. "All clear," she said. "Unload at will."

"Happy to oblige," came Sorrel's clear, high voice.

Yup. She was going to keep the Oligochuno. The others, though…

"Want to see what trouble we can get into?" Judit asked Saxon with a sly grin.

Saxon didn't quite roll his eyes at her. Almost, though. "Shall we instead bring up our bill of lading and get the goods to our customer?"

"Yeah, fine," Judit said. She unbuckled herself out of her pilot's chair and stood up, stretching her one hundred seventy centimeter frame. Maybe in a year or so she could replace that damned chair. It really wasn't as comfortable as her chair in *Levente*. She should have thought to bring it along.

"Perhaps we shall find a spot of trouble later," Saxon added with a broad wink.

Judit grinned up at him. Neither of them had ever been to *Mawar* station before. The bad parts of the space station shouldn't be that hard to find, though.

Humming, Judit made her way out of the main helm, down the long corridor to the hatch that was still cycling open.

The dock had forty landing pads. About a third of them had ships parked there. Judit was surprised at how quiet it was when she stepped out onto the solid metal floor—only a few ships' crews were actively loading or unloading. The rest of the ships stood silent. Maybe they'd arrived during the station's "night?" She'd have to check.

Though it could also be the fact that the ceiling of the dock rose up forever, possibly eighteen meters high. Wow. Did they get such huge ships in here sometimes?

The air smelled right, of machine oil and shaved metal. One of the closest ships was having work done to its exterior. Small repair bots crawled all over it. They looked like mechanical crabs, each a bit larger than her outstretched hand. Individually, none of them had much computing power. But when they worked in a swarm, they could solve problems easily. In the quiet of the dock, she could just make out the clicking of their claws across the ship's hull.

Judit allowed herself a huge smile as she started walking away from the ship. The gravity was set at what Humans referred to as "Earth normal." She tended to keep her ships set to the same, while each crew member could lighten or strengthen the gravity in their own cabins as they saw fit.

No one stood waiting for her with a clipboard at the

ready. That sort of service was only available for more important ships, or ones who flew for the Cartel.

While the center of the dock was filled with landing pads and ships, the edges were clearly marked walkways. Judit followed the easy-to-read yellow signs, pointing her toward the station's customs office. One side of the dock was open to space, protected from it by an invisible "curtain." Judit had parked next to the opening more than once. It had always filled her with a sense of vertigo, irrationally afraid that the system would fail and she'd be sucked out.

The customs office was located in the interior of the dock, toward where a person entered into the station itself. The office was merely a desk with a Bantel sitting behind it, surrounded by tall plastic walls that enclosed the space, reaching all the way to the top of the incredibly high ceiling.

If there was some sort of accident, would those walls protect the occupants? Probably. She didn't think that any of the pilots would get rowdy and that the official needed protection from beam weapons. Though you never knew. Maybe those walls were beam-proof as well, the plastic distorting any sort of beam weapon just enough to lessen the effect.

Judit had left her gun back on the ship, of course. *Mawar* station was supposedly a civilized place. She'd been in more than one system where everyone went armed all the time. It just depended.

Two pilots stood in front of her, one Human, one Yu'udir. Judit fidgeted where she stood.

Come *on.* She didn't have that many hours on her contract left.

She pulled out the i-stick that contained her bill of lading, along with all the other information about her ship.

The i-stick for the ship fit comfortably into the palm of her hand. It was an older model, so slightly more than five centimeters across. Hard silver-metal nubs covered the center barrel, while the ends glowed with bright green rings. *Ferdinand II Information Stick* was stamped in the middle of it.

She looked back toward her ship while she waited. Saxon was helping Sorrel with the unloading. Xidong, Brett, and the others appeared to be helping as well.

There was a coffee and tea kiosk over in the far corner. It also appeared to be selling donuts, or the Bantel equivalent. Cultures who ate grain generally figured out ways to deep fry it. A few Cartel guards stood at the front of the large space, wearing heavy armor, their facemasks blackened: two Humans and one Khanvassa, who was twice as wide and probably four times as formidable as the Humans.

When Judit looked back toward her ship, she watched an official with a scanner come walking up. He wore the solid navy-blue uniform of the Cartel, with a high stiff collar, long sleeves, long pants, and black boots. Judit hadn't seen many of the Bantel in a single, solid color before. Mind you, his skin was a bright, light blue. Possibly it was a sort of, "up yours" gesture. More likely, the Bantel thought the colors went together. Which they did not.

Judit looked back over at the official behind the desk. There was now only one other pilot in line in front of her. Good.

Maybe she should stop and get donuts for everyone, after she finished filling out all the paperwork. It would be a nice gesture, though it might also be a nice "goodbye" for most of them.

Huh. There appeared to be a problem back at her ship. The official had stepped back and gestured for other officials to step forward.

Now, guards were coming forward. Aggressively. Why were they pointing their long riffles at Saxon?

What the hell?

Judit started walking rapidly back toward the quickly escalating conflict, though the official behind her yelled at her to stay put.

However, Judit had never backed down from conflict. While other people might freeze, or go get help, Judit always raced into the thick of things.

It was a trait her mother said would get her killed one of these days.

Hopefully, today wasn't that day.

CHAPTER 4

XIDONG

XIDONG COULDN'T HELP but drum his fingers against the table in front of him, a habit from playing game consoles too long. While he could keep his body still, his hands and his fingers just had to keep moving. It was a Human thing. He'd met Bantel players who, while they could keep their hands still, would have a constant moving flush around their neck ruff that showed their addiction.

Yu'udir tended to just growl a lot.

He'd been separated from the others the crew of *Ferdinand II.* While he suspected that this was standard procedure, it still made him nervous.

There was no reason for him to be nervous though, right? He'd done what they'd asked him to do…

The room was plain, the walls painted an industrial gray, with a cold metal table that he tapped his fingers against, a cold metal chair that his butt couldn't seem to warm, and a cold concrete floor that was probably easy to wash, to clean off any blood that got spilt. The air smelled stale, as if the filters hadn't been changed regularly. Xidong himself might have come in here smelling of stale sweat, but that had faded.

He'd never been in a room like this before. Not in real life. In one of his stim games, sure. It was always like this. Single light fixture in a cage above his head. One way mirror across the wall in front of him. Bad guys surely behind it.

Xidong would admit that he looked tired. And quite possibly scared, though he kept telling himself that he didn't have to be afraid. He kept his black bangs cut shorter than he'd like, so they wouldn't quite fall into his eyes. He had to work for a living, and while the longer cut made him look more like a sexy bad boy and not like the geek he was at heart, it was a pain in the ass to always have to shove it out of the way.

Even in the dim mirror he could see his Asian heritage, the fold above the eye, his skin a golden color and not the white, black, or even red-tinged hue of the rest of the Humans.

He wore a plain gray long-sleeved shirt and black pants, something meant to make him stand out less. No one was supposed to notice him or pay any attention to him.

In the real world.

In the game world, he had quite a reputation for insanity, for taking wacked out chances and frequently winning as a result. He'd lost track of the number of bets he'd won by taking the nonobvious choice.

The times that his luck had failed, when he'd ended up in debt, well, he was about to make up for all of those, wasn't he?

He couldn't help but jump when the door behind him banged open. A Yu'udir came striding in. She wore a greenish-yellow tweed vest with a matching flat cap and carried a large leather briefcase.

She placed the case on the table lightly and came to stand on the other side. "Xidong Han Chin, you have been arrested for traveling on the ship *Ferdinand II*, which was found to be smuggling illegal hallucinogenics," she said in a very serious voice.

Xidong gulped and merely nodded. They weren't about to charge him with the others, were they? He'd been paid by the Cartel to *put* those drugs on the ship in the first place!

The Yu'udir gave him a sly smile. "However, I've been told that you have a get out of jail free card. Is that correct?" She popped open the briefcase and pulled out an i-stick. The side of it must have had some sort of display, given how it slightly glowed.

"Yes, yes ma'am," Xidong said. "I have a contact number."

He'd memorized the number so he wouldn't have to carry it with him, and also so no one could find it. He recited the number to the Yu'udir, who appeared to be comparing the number he said with the one on the i-stick she held.

She nodded, putting the i-stick back in her briefcase, then nodded at him. After a pause, she closed her briefcase. "As far as I'm concerned, you're free to go."

"That's it?" Xidong said. He tensed his legs getting ready to stand. "No further demands?" He'd been expecting that the Cartel would try to blackmail him into doing further work for them.

Not that he wanted to do this sort of thing again. Though the money was awfully good…

The Yu'udir gave him a toothy grin, sharp white teeth making a sudden appearance in her black face. "No, no, we don't work that way. See, you're an addict."

Xidong flinched. He wasn't addicted to his games! He could quit at any time.

Though in his heart of hearts he knew the Yu'udir was right. He might be able to quit the game at any time. The side bets, though, that high from winning all that money? That might be much more difficult to walk away from.

"And as an addict, you'll be back. You need us much more than we need you," she added just before she swept out of the room.

Xidong shivered. He forgot sometimes how quietly the Yu'udir could move. Silently at speed, as a matter of fact. They'd learned how as the apex predators of their home planet, and had never lost that skill.

More than just the Yu'udir made up the Cartel. All the races were represented there.

However, they were sharks. And he was just a little fish.

Xidong stood up in the cold room and shivered once. He was determined to walk away and never look back.

He knew he was lying even as he crossed the threshold, already salivating for that next big score.

CHAPTER 5

JUDIT

"No, I was not smuggling hallucinogenics, illegal or otherwise," Judit told the stupid Human official sitting in front of her. Again.

This room might have been meant to intimidate people —dark gray cinder block walls, cold metal table and chair, hard floor and glaring light, one-way mirror against the far wall.

It had just made her angrier. As well as more determined to make sure this fool understood that she'd been set up. And no, she didn't know by whom. Probably someone on the new crew. Hell, for all she knew it was that damned Bantel Brett, who was always so cheerful.

Never trust anyone who smiled that much.

"If you'll just look at my record, you'll see that I have never had so much as a warning for smuggling," Judit pointed out. She had a clean record when it came to transporting cargo. She'd turned down plenty of potential work that skirted the law. As an independent, she took pride in finding her own damned work and doing her job well.

"Maybe you were just never caught before," the official

said. He was a flabby man, with jowls that would probably flap in low gravity, small beady eyes that probably needed the glaring light in order to see even two centimeters in front of his fat nose, thin lips with lines around the edges that curved downward, showing that his expression was always sour. The bright light did nothing for his pale white skin, except highlight the grease accumulated across his forehead and along the sides of his nose.

"I've never been caught because I've never done anything wrong," Judit insisted. "I was set up."

She leaned back in her chair so she wouldn't reach out and try to slap some sense into this idiot. She knew she'd lose if she did. They hadn't handcuffed her to the table, but that had been a close call, given how she'd been shouting at the stupid guards.

She was slowly losing it. Along with her patience.

And when that went, her ship was probably lost to her as well.

"But who would set you—" The official didn't get to finish that thought as the door behind Judit swung open.

A Yu'udir female loomed in the opening. She wore a stylish greenish-yellow tweed vest with a matching flat cap and carried a large leather briefcase. Saxon would have rocked that look. As it was, this Yu'udir merely looked professorial.

"Might I have a word?" she asked in a melodious voice.

Interesting. The official in front of Judit paled further. Who was this Yu'udir and whom did she represent?

The official gulped, stood up, and quickly scurried out.

"So who are you, that you can make the office mice squeak that way?" Judit asked the newcomer.

"I am Agnes," the Yu'udir said, placing her briefcase on the table between them. "It appears that you're in something of a mess."

Judit snorted. "Ya think?" She sat back in her chair and faked a nice, loose, easygoing posture.

While she wasn't a poker player, she knew how to bargain better than most Humans, who expected prices to be written down as well as fair.

Whereas Judit had learned how to bargain at her mama's knee. It was one of the few forms of sport that you could get on the small station where she'd grown up.

"My employers have empowered me to make people such as yourself an offer. One that would be better than being placed on the planet below, in a prison," Agnes said.

"Lay it on me," Judit said, keeping her smile rather than showing the shiver of horror she felt.

Being planet-bound? Oh, gods no. She'd drop herself down a garbage chute and send her body out into the vacuum of space before she'd allow herself to be stuck on a planet for the rest of her life, having to deal with *weather* and other atrocities.

"The Universal Trading Cartel is always on the lookout for good pilots, such as yourself," Agnes said smoothly.

Judit couldn't help but feel her eyes widen. It wasn't a huge tell, but she knew it was enough. Any sharp player—and Agnes was definitely both sharp and a player—would know how surprised Judit was.

Shit. The Cartel was behind this setup? Judit felt her throat go dry, as if all the blowers on the station had lit up to send some stench to the far corners. The room wasn't getting any smaller, but she wouldn't swear that the walls hadn't crept in a few centimeters. Though Judit had been hungry before, thinking about those Bantel donuts, now her stomach churned as if she'd had too much coffee before any protein.

Judit let Agnes say her spiel uninterrupted. May as well get all the bad news out and on the table at one time.

They'd provide her with a ship, of course, since *Ferdinand*

II was now forfeit. Agnes didn't spell out that Judit's wages would be garnished forever trying to pay back that new ship, though Judit knew that was what the contract would say.

Judit would have her choice of runs. However, all of them would be long.

A short run between a station and a gate was acceptable. Short runs lasted from hours to days. A long run meant months on a spaceship, with the same crew, having to travel from the only available gate in a system to the first inhabitable planet. (Why folks chose to live out in the boonies like that never made a damned bit of sense to her.)

Judit didn't like herself enough, let alone any other being, to spend months with them living on top of one another in close quarters. Probably no one other than herself would survive the first long run.

"Would I have to admit guilt of smuggling?" was the first question Judit could think to ask, instead of screaming at the top of her lungs, *Are you fucking kidding me???*

"All of this unpleasantness would be expunged from your record," Agnes assured her.

Uh huh. Sure. Judit didn't believe it for a second. The Cartel would hold onto those records to keep her in line.

"What about the rest of my crew?" Judit said. That was her next concern. She didn't really care about the others, but Saxon had been with her for years.

"I'll see whether or not I can get my employer to make them similar deals," Agnes said smoothly.

Judit assumed that meant, "No way in hell," in polite speak.

"You've given me a tremendous amount to think about," Judit assured Agnes. "But I'm going to need some time to mull it over."

Which was her polite way of saying, "No way in hell."

Judit had been around Saxon long enough to see the

surprise that crossed Agnes's face. Obviously, the Yu'udir wasn't used to people turning her down.

Too bad.

"Don't take too long," Agnes warned as she stood up. "This offer won't last once your hearing starts."

"Which would be…?"

Agnes stopped just inside the door. "Tomorrow," she said firmly.

Judit nodded, showing she'd understood.

She had just a single day to find her way out of this damned trap.

And not a single clue how.

CHAPTER 6

JUDIT

JUDIT PACED AROUND the small gray room, trying to find a way out.

She was trapped, and she knew it. This wasn't between a rock and a hard place. No, this was a choice between two hells, neither of which she had any chance of surviving.

Being planet-bound. Having to deal with *weather*. Let alone being trapped in a cage, in a prison.

And she'd thought her home station had been bad. Prison would be worse.

On the other hand, there were the long runs that she'd be forced to do. Same people, day in, day out. Same damned run. Always in debt to the Cartel. It was polite slavery. She'd be just as trapped taking that option.

There had to be another way out.

"Excuse me," came a voice from the wall.

Judit started. Then backed up all the way across the room when a piece of the wall broke away and came toward her.

Shit. Had she already gone completely mad? Her heart pounded like crazy. Sweat started gathering under her arms and her palms grew clammy.

No, that wasn't the wall talking to her. It was a damned Bantel, who'd been camouflaged, hiding, pressed up against the wall.

His clothing maintained that same gray cinder-block look, while his exposed skin changed, growing pink. He blinked and his eyes changed color as well, going from gray to bright yellow.

Of course, if he was wearing neutral gray colored clothing, the color of his skin and his eyes had to clash. Or something.

"Who the hell are you and what do you want?" Judit asked after taking a deep breath and trying to calm herself.

The Bantel was shorter than she, as most were. He had a broad nose that took up most of his face, under his bulging yellow eyes. His mouth was hidden under that nose, but Judit would bet that he was smiling. As the Bantel usually were.

This one had broad shoulders, as if he'd been lifting weights. Or heavy guns. His arms were more muscled than most Bantels as well. The tips of his long, skinny fingers ended in tiny suction cups. Most Bantel could no longer use them for climbing walls, though she suspected the one in front of her could.

"My name is Fran, and I have a different proposition for you," he said.

Judit sighed. She knew she wasn't going to like this one any better than the other two.

"All right," she said after a moment. Might as well add a third hell to the two already in front of her.

"My employer builds experimental spaceships," Fran said. "We want to hire you to fly them."

Judit blinked, waiting a few moments for the other shoe to drop. When that appeared to be the whole of Fran's pitch, she asked, "What's the catch?"

"While we take every precaution, these are *experimental* ships," Fran said.

Judit nodded, finally piecing the implications together. "Not all your crews survive," she guessed.

Yup. Meet hell number three. Though this one was a tad less awful, all things considered.

"It's only been a few," Fran assured her. "However, my employer makes certain that your beneficiaries are well taken care of, if an accident occurs."

"That's nice of them," Judit said, trying to keep at least some of the sarcasm at bay. "What about my crew?"

Fran blinked sets of his eyelids. The neon yellow grew hazy. All the Bantel had more than one set of eyelids. Judit guessed that Fran had replaced a natural one with some sort of screen.

Interesting. Not many people among any of the species were bio-enhanced. It wasn't socially accepted.

Whoever Fran's employer was, they had to be awfully mellow if they allowed that sort of thing in their employees.

"You do realize that one of your crew turned you in?" Fran said.

"Do you know who?" Judit asked. She'd bet it was that damned Brett.

"I'll see if I can find that information out," Fran said. He paused, his eyes rapidly scanning back and forth, as if searching for something. "Ah. Saxon is the only other member of your crew who's still being held. All the rest were released."

That made sense if the Cartel was looking for trained recruits. While Sorrel, her cargo master, had enough skill to impress her, the rest hadn't.

"First off, if you want to recruit me, you will also have to take Saxon," Judit said firmly. They were a package deal.

"Next, you have to let me speak to him, before I make a decision."

Fran blinked again, his eyes suddenly clear.

"Let me see what I can do," he said, not making any promises.

The i-stick he pulled out of a hidden pocket worked its magic on the door, and Fran slipped out.

A moment later, Fran popped his head back through the door. "Aren't you coming?"

Judit blinked, surprised. "Aren't I still a prisoner?" she said.

"No one will notice you," Fran assured her. "Just walk as though you know what you're doing. Come on. We gotta go see Saxon."

Judit took a deep breath, then released it.

What the hell.

Option number three might have been as much of a dead end as the others, just a much shorter one.

She slipped out of the room, following Fran, hoping that the god of fools would keep smiling at her for a while longer.

CHAPTER 7

SAXON

SAXON, like the rest of the Yu'udir, didn't have a fantastic sense of smell. Their ancestors had tracked their prey by sight and movement rather than by odor.

However, there was a faint trace of...something, remaining in the air after Agnes had left. A sweet scent, perhaps floral in nature.

Was that meant to entice him on an unconscious level?

Certainly, he and Agnes had hit it off, as it were. Compadres, facing a difficult situation together. If only Saxon would allow Agnes to help him out!

Except that Saxon had a sneaking suspicion that Agnes, or rather her employers, had been the ones to put Saxon and Judit in this impossible situation in the first place.

Saxon didn't care much for the interview room they'd left him in. It was monochrome in nature—light gray walls, bright metal table, dark gray concrete floor. Plus, the chair was not suited for a Yu'udir in the slightest. At least it wasn't too warm.

Saxon's brown tweed vest, like most of the tweed vests that his species wore, contained a cooling unit. The Yu'udir had learned early on that they were the only species who preferred a much cooler climate. They'd adapted by creating special vests that helped them stay comfortable.

That his vests were primarily tweed helped convey the image the Yu'udir wanted to present—that of some sort of teacher or specialist. The caps that Saxon and the others wore normally also contained a cooling gel pack.

After speaking with Agnes and hearing her spiel, Saxon had insisted on reading the contract in detail before he'd agree to anything. Agnes had been prepared for that, of course. It was what any Yu'udir would do. She wouldn't leave a copy with him, though. What, was she afraid that he'd use it to somehow fold it into a weapon, or us it open the door and slip out of there?

There were several clauses that he was certain he could renegotiate, such as the type of ship he would serve on, the accommodations, and so on.

There were other parts that he knew he wouldn't be able to adjust. Such as the long run clauses, as well as how the Cartel would take "training fees" out of his regular wages.

Which meant that every time he changed ships, or crews, whatever savings he'd accumulated would be wiped out.

Though it wasn't explicit in the contract, he knew that the Cartel would ensure that he'd never end up on the same space station as Judit again. That, too, stuck in his fangs, some nasty bit that he just couldn't seem to floss away.

Agnes had politely ignored his requests to see Judit, her "I'll see what I can do," easily read as, "Not until the heat death of the universe."

However, Saxon would not abandon his companion. Could he add a clause that put them on the same ship? The Cartel would never go for it. They wanted him isolated. As well as her.

A single soul working against the immense Cartel would

be quickly overwhelmed. Two souls might be as well, but at least they could support each other. Maybe get others to join them.

His choices were to betray the very nature of his soul, by leaving a true comrade behind, or be forced into hard labor in a prison on the planet below. A planet that Agnes assured him was regularly thirty-five degrees. Or higher.

When the door opened, Saxon braced himself for another round of verbal sparring.

He could have been knocked over by a snowflake when Judit came sneaking in.

It surprised him further when she came straight over to him and wrapped her arms around him in a fierce hug.

Of course, he returned it more decorously. Though Humans were tough, the Yu'udir were much stronger.

The sentiment was the same, though, as he hugged her back.

"Are you all right?" she asked, pulling back and looking up at him, searching his face for any signs of discomfort.

"I'm fine," he assured her. She'd patched him up after a few bar fights, so she knew what to look for.

No punches had been thrown. No, they wanted him trapped in his head, not fighting his way out.

She nodded, as if she heard his internal growling. "I know," she said. "Just barely managed not to slap one of those officials myself."

Saxon nodded as Judit took a step back. "How did you manage to free yourself?"

"I didn't," Judit grimaced. "I had help." She sighed. "There's a Bantel offering me—us—a job opportunity."

"Go on," Saxon said. He wasn't certain that he was going to like this any more than the other two "offers" he'd already received.

"It involves flying experimental spaceships," Judit said. "The catch is that not all crews survive these 'experiments.'"

"I see," Saxon said. And he did.

While Judit didn't see herself as anything special, Saxon knew her belief was incorrect.

Most spaceships, at least the cargo carriers that Judit preferred, were fully automated. They barely needed a pilot, just a course plotted out.

The *Levente* had been older. Judit had learned to fly the ship, not just how to set a course.

He suspected that she never would have been happy with *Ferdinand II*, as it was like piloting a cruise ship through clear waters. Judit much preferred a small sled flying over the ice, fast and maneuverable.

Judit didn't understand that part of the reason why the Cartel was trying to recruit her was because she *could* fly a ship. That perfectly controlled, manual landing she'd done on the deck of *Mawar* had probably sent frissons of fear through all the decks.

The Cartel didn't want pilots operating on their own. It wanted nice little cogs to fit into their machine.

"I would take it," Saxon said after a moment. "Always take the easy tunnel," he reminded her. It was a saying among those who lived in spaceships—the easy tunnel through hyperspace was *always* the right choice.

Judit shook her head. "Not without you."

Saxon had to smile at that. While it was well known that the Yu'udir were faithful to their companions, sometimes to a fault, Humans could be more capricious.

Not his pilot, though.

"Of course, not without me," Saxon said in his driest tone. "Who else would back you up at the next bar fight?"

Judit rolled her eyes at him. "I'm not always the one who starts those fights. Just saying."

"If you insist," Saxon said, not budging an centimeter.

"Fine," Judit said. "Let's go get Fran. And blow this popsicle joint."

"Indeed," Saxon said.

He wondered again at that faint odor that still remained in the room, that threaded through his nose as they left.

Had he turned down a possible romantic liaison by following his captain, this Human, instead?

Possibly so. Possibly not.

But that was in the past, a door closed as firmly as if a mountain had risen up in front of it.

His future might end in a big bang. It was still a better way to go.

CHAPTER 8

CLAYTON

CLAYTON SLIDELL PAUSED after dessert had been consumed, considering his dinner companions, all of them directors of some sort for The Universal Trading Cartel. Seven of the eight were Humans, himself included, with a single Oligochuno, Rosemary, joining them. He hadn't chosen all of his companions: some of them were just along for the ride.

And though the history books would never know about this group or this meeting, or be able to understand the consequences of a supposedly trivial get-together, Clayton knew that here, now, was the start of his true legacy.

He pushed his chair back from the table, signaling that the meal was over and it was time to proceed to other things. The eight of them rose as one and made their way from the dining room to the study.

Faux wood stained nearly black made up the bar along the far wall of the study, as well as the trim throughout the room. Thick gray carpet that cushioned every step covered the floor. Human couches and chairs took up much of the space, all done in tasteful beiges and browns. A bookshelf filled with serious looking tomes covered the wall to the left of the door, while the entire wall to the right was filled with floor to ceiling windows.

The view looked out on what appeared to be a dark, stormy ocean at night. Moonlight highlighted the foamy white tops, and the wind whistled as it blew past. You could practically smell the salt in the air.

However, the "view" was just a projection. They were actually located on the space station *Fausto*, in the Copernicus system. If you tried to open one of the windows and step out, you'd run straight into a bulkhead.

Clayton would have preferred an open prairie, covered with dried grass and sage brush, painted hills in the background, and maybe a couple of herds of cattle grazing in the distance.

The storm might better fit what would be coming, though.

The bar was stocked with just about every booze, narcotic, or knock-out juice any damned species could want. The Universal Trading Cartel club reserved the best for those directors with A class stocks, that is, those who could vote.

Clayton noted those who headed straight for the bar for an after-dinner drink, and those who didn't. While most settled for a traditional scotch or whiskey, Rosemary, the Oligochuno, had to have something disgustingly pink and probably addictive.

Clayton didn't know why the damned worms insisted on using Human spices for their names. Some sort of in-joke, he was certain, as Oligochunos used scent to communicate far more than any other species. Each of their clans came with their own odor. Everyone knew that you should never ask about an Oligochuno's family—not unless you were prepared for the stench.

After fetching zir drink, Rosemary disdained any of the

Human couches. Zie flattened out zir tail behind zim and leaned back on it, looking comfortable enough.

Zie seemed to understand that something was up, as zie raised her glass to Clayton then "sat" quietly, waiting for the others to catch up.

Not all of the directors could come to this club. Only those with a certain percentage of voting stock.

In other words, only those who *counted*.

It wasn't always the case that a single species dominated one of these casual dinners of the directors. Clayton could think of more than one occasion when he'd been the only Human.

He hadn't specifically arranged tonight's meeting. It had been more of a suggestion, passed along certain channels.

That the crew tonight happened to contain some of the most aggressive directors was just a coincidence. Honest.

As people finished topping off their beverages, Clayton surveyed the group. Sharks, every one of them. Rosemary was actually sharper than most. They might hide their teeth well, but the Oligochuno were well known for their vicious negotiation tactics.

Just who he needed.

There was the usual chatter about trade. Who was bribing who in order to try to start another damned war. Rumors of shortages and what Universal could do about it, both with and without a profit.

That was one of the superpowers of Universal. It kept track of every damned detail, then it *planned*. Clayton had read enough history to understand that had been the downfall of so many empires back on Earth: the inability to see beyond next quarter's profits.

Universal had been set up from the start to encourage long-term thinking. Not merely a year, but ten and twenty-five years out. It was why it was the most successful of all the intergalactic organizations so far.

It helped that Universal controlled all the hyperspace gates. The tunnels were a natural phenomenon, predicted in most systems by physics. However, no one could enter a tunnel without passing a Universal checkpoint.

Of course, the checkpoints closer to the center of inhabited space were run with integrity. It was only out on the edges where things got more hinky. You couldn't keep all the graft and bribery out of the system. It was just too damned big. You could only try to control it. Maybe have a few surprise inspections, make a corrupt system pay out a huge fine.

But that was about all that Universal could realistically do.

Eventually, Clayton joined in the conversation, steering it like an unwieldy tug pulling a cruise ship three times its size. It took some time, but he had all night.

Finally, he saw his opening, and he asked about the latest sightings of the Chonchu, and whether or not Universal needed to raise the fees that the bugs had to pay to leave their system.

Since they were a hive mind, the Chonchu couldn't travel singly. They needed to stay in groups of between three to five to maintain a semblance of consciousness.

"Those things just leave me cold," Clayton said with an exaggerated shudder. Though the sentiment was real, his reaction wasn't. Not really.

He'd just as soon go into that system with enough bombs to destroy every single one of their planets. But they'd never actually proven themselves to be enough of a threat to justify that sort of action.

Yet.

"I know, right?" Malina said. She wore an awfully bright

orange sari with some sort of red, short top underneath. Gold and red dots had been stuck to her forehead, like one of those statues he'd seen in a museum. She had a gold ring in her nose, with a chain that hung across her cheek to her ear, like half a bridle or something. Either she'd had work done, or her light brown skin hid her wrinkles really well. She wore a bright red shade of lipstick that appeared to make her mouth three times as big as it normally was. It wasn't a good look.

Despite all that, Malina was one of the first people who Clayton had reached out to, inviting her to come to that evening's meal. She excelled at excess and always wanted more of everything. This made her ruthless when it came to making a profit. "Profit over people," she'd been quoted saying more than once.

"They look like walking, talking fish," Rodrigo added. He gave a nasty laugh, the kind he was known for. "Makes me want to get out my filleting knife. Trim one up for dinner."

Rodrigo had been second or third on Clayton's prospective list. While his dining habits might leave something to be desired, he made an excellent packager when it came to putting together people and pallets. He wore a starched white shirt, a black tuxedo jacket with tails, as well as a satin purple sash. Supposedly he was some sort of royalty from whatever backwards Mexican planet that he'd grown up on.

Small fish in an even smaller pond.

"You know who's been welcoming the damned bugs? Arthur Pendragon," Clayton said.

"Oh, please. Arthur and his *Camelot*," Rosemary said. Like most of the Oligochuno, zie didn't bother with clothes. Rosemary's sides were particularly lumpy instead, as zie had grown internal pockets for whatever it was they needed to carry. "He's isolated there, with delusions of his own importance and grandeur."

"I disagree," Stormy said. She was the youngest of the group, and the flashiest, in a silver sequined gown that plunged down to her navel and was probably held up with boob tape and glue. She had the figure for it, an hourglass shape that only the best plastic surgeons could maintain.

However, as the youngest, she had a different way of approaching things. Frequently, her ideas were stupid and immature. Sometimes Clayton just wanted to slap her. However, every once in a while she had moments of chilling clarity, like waking up beside a kitten who'd turned into a lion overnight.

Behind all that glitz and glam was a first-class brain. If she'd only allow herself to use it more often, rather than her boobs.

"I think Arthur is dangerous because he's an *idealist*," Stormy added. "We all know how impractical it is to actually own a space station."

Several in the group nodded. Much better to lease such a huge property than to actually own it and be responsible for damages as well as maintenance. While it was possible to be something of a slum lord when it came to a space station, you had to keep the damned things running, which meant you were always pumping money into them.

Much better to have a third party keep that headache.

"He gives the illusion of freedom," Stormy continued. "It's an ideal that others can hope for. Dream for. Agitate for."

Clayton along with several of the others nodded. It wasn't that people weren't free. They were. However, they also needed to get along with each other as well as with the other species.

Universal and the board were not in charge of all the

worlds. It only felt that way sometimes, with Universal being the supreme leader trying to direct seventeen hundred squabbling minor kings with delusions of relevance.

Without Universal, there would be chaos. Simple as that. Clayton was determined to not let that happen on his watch.

Which was one of the other reasons why people like Arthur were so dangerous. Along with the damned bugs.

What would the universe look like if just anyone could create a tunnel, then go flying into or out of any system they damned well chose?

Wars would break out instantly. No, you needed a nice, ordered system. Usually, Universal didn't allow troop transports. There was a time and a place for it, of course. If a big enough bribe was met.

However, the damned Chonchu had been fairly technologically advanced by the time Universal had found them about two hundred years ago. Not only had they discovered the existence of the hyperspace tunnels, they were in the process of figuring out how to create their own.

That was just never going to be allowed.

Fortunately, they were a hive mind, reliant on queens who controlled large areas. It was easy to build up fears among the other species of being taken over or dominated by a single species. Then, it appeared a plague took their system, destroyed almost all of their queens. Or at least that was the official story that Clayton's grandfather had told him. Made the bugs dependent on Universal for delivering things.

And Clayton intended to keep it that way.

"So how would you storm a castle?" he asked. He gave the group a huge grin. "Take out a place like *Camelot*?"

The others caught onto the game quickly, throwing out ridiculous suggestions like introducing a metal-eating virus as well as closing the tunnels nearby, so while you could get to the station, you'd never be able to leave.

Malina finally added, "I wouldn't do anything at all. I'd have someone else do something."

"Who, my dear?" Clayton asked. They'd finally gotten to the part of the evening that he was sincerely interested in.

"Oh, I don't know," Malina said. She waved one elegant hand in the air. "That's something for my *people* to know. Not anything I have to sully my hands with." She speared him with a hard look. "Get your people to talk to mine. I'm sure they can suggest someone."

"Or you could just get a pirate crew of Yu'udir to attack the station," someone else added.

"Now, why didn't I think of that?" Clayton exclaimed, sitting back, letting the game continue.

No one would remember this conversation after the evening had passed. Not even when something *did* happen to *Camelot*.

Or if they did remember, they'd also know that it was best to not cross Clayton. In case that sort of thing needed to be repeated, and might happen to them next.

CHAPTER 9

SAXON

POSSIBLY, it shouldn't have surprised Saxon at how quickly Fran had been able to extricate Judit and himself from the *Mawar* station. It had taken mere hours, and not days, once they'd successfully negotiated a contract between the three of them.

Still, Saxon found himself at something of a loss as they hurtled out of the Kembag system and into the closest gate, out of the system.

He hadn't been at either helm of the ship to hear the communications it had with the gate guards, those tyrants set in place by the Cartel. However, it seemed to him that the ship had some sort of priority clearance, as they went directly through the gate without much of a pause.

Now, Saxon stood in the forward lounge. The room itself had a sterile feeling to it, with couches and chairs that appeared to fit most species, done in neutral colors. Dim light came from the ceiling, a relaxing glow. Maybe six Yu'udir could fit comfortably in the area, which would mean perhaps a dozen Humans, or merely three of the Khanvassa.

The windows that filled the front wall, as well as the

entire wall opposite the door, dominated the space. They went from mid-way up the wall and rose to the ceiling, and were filled with what one could see of hyperspace.

The view was primarily that of a night sky, with fixed pinpoints of light whose placement never changed, regardless of how fast the ship went. Scientists theorized that the points were actually part of the tunnel that traveled with you as you moved, but no one knew for certain. The placement of the fixed lights changed with every trip. The lounge was on the starboard side of the ship, and there were a trio of bright lights just past center, on the port side. Another handful of bright lights along with an uncountable number of dim ones seemed to be riding just to the port side of the ship.

Additional blips of light passed, sometimes directly in front of the ship, other times on a side. Those were either large systems that the ship was sailing past, or they were other ships in hyperspace. The lights naturally repelled each other, so unless you had a suicidal madwoman at the helm, ships wouldn't collide.

Then there were the occasional polychromatic clouds which lay across the path that a ship would pass through, here and gone. No one knew what caused those to appear. Of course, scientists had theories, but no one seemed to be able to agree on what caused the spectacle.

The phenomenon was almost impossible to study. If you slowed a ship too far, you'd pop out of hyperspace, generally with your ship crushed to bits, as if you'd gone into the depths of an ocean. Scientists flew special ships covered in sensors through the clouds, then would argue for years about what the data meant.

The Khanvassa believed that they were trails of their spider goddess, evidence that She had passed recently.

Saxon merely delighted in the glow of colors that washed over his fur as the ship passed through one.

"Damn it! I missed it," came Judit's voice from behind.

Saxon looked at her from over his shoulder. She looked slightly less manic now that they'd left the Kembag system. She wore her usual loose-fitting shirt, that day, burgundy, along with much tighter fitting black pants. All of it could be easily squished into a spacesuit if life support failed.

As she was dressed so somberly, Saxon had taken it upon himself to provide a spot of color, so his tweed vest was screaming yellow, which he'd been told went well with his white fur and blue eyes.

Judit gave him a smile that at least looked real. Like him, she'd been worried that they might be caught or stopped.

They weren't free, not by a long shot. But at least they'd managed to leave the first trap.

What kind of fangs and claws the next had was yet to be determined.

"There might be more clouds later," Saxon told her as she came to stand beside him.

Judit shrugged. "Wouldn't want to use up my luck wishing for something like that. Not when we might need a lot more luck later."

Saxon nodded. He didn't necessarily agree with Judit that luck, like endurance, was only available in limited quantities. Judit took her luck seriously though.

"I spent some time looking up *Camelot* and Arthur," Judit said quietly.

Ah, that was why she hadn't joined him immediately after launch in the observation lounge.

"Did you learn anything useful?" Saxon asked after a few moments of companionable silence.

"He's a bit of an idealist," Judit said. "Supposedly, all are welcome at *Camelot*. Even if you arrive without a credit to your name you'll be allowed on the station and provided employment."

"Do you think it's like the *Kohza* station?" Saxon mused.

Judit shuddered, as he'd thought she might. *Kohza* had had the same sort of policy, where all would be greeted with open arms. However, it had turned out that instead of useful jobs, there were four people assigned to every tourist, there to make sure the tourist was gently parted from all the credits they'd arrived with.

"*Szar*, I hope not," Judit said.

It was never a good sign when Judit was swearing in Hungarian. It meant she was still very much on edge.

But there was nothing either of them could do about it. Not until they actually reached the station and the next part of their journey.

CHAPTER 10

JUDIT

A<small>LTHOUGH</small> J<small>UDIT HAD</small> hopes of grungy back corridors and places to easily get lost in, *Camelot*, at least from a distance, appeared all clean and shiny and *new*. It was composed of seven distinct circles running around a solid core. She would have called it bland, except for the color.

Who painted their space station bright gold?

Most space stations were the plain silver of steel, maybe with some white or black accents.

Camelot shone like a second sun, warm and welcoming.

It was weird, but nice.

She exchanged a puzzled look with Saxon, but neither of them said anything. At least he looked as confused as she felt.

The pilot drove them straight into a docking pad, one with room enough for a couple dozen ships.

Fran came to collect them in the forward lounge. He'd ditched the gray cinderblock shirt for a truly eye-searing pink-and-white striped shirt, with pants that stopped just above his knee in a clashing orange-red. To top that off, his skin was now lime green.

Judit wondered if Fran was meant to inspire visions without hallucinogenics.

"We have just a little more paperwork to finish up," he said cheerfully.

Of course. Stupid Bantels were always happy. Probably did a little dance when they pronounced someone's death.

He handed them both an i-stick. It was gold—the same damned color as the exterior of the station. It was a slender tube, maybe about as big in diameter as Judit's pinky finger. However, it was only about as long as her palm.

"This will get you around the station, open appropriate doors in the dock, and so on," Fran said.

When Judit pressed the top of the i-stick, a small clip jutted out. She slid the i-stick up along the collar of her shirt. Saxon stuck his in a pocket of his vest.

"Your i-stick contains your first month's credits as well as a signing bonus," Fran added. "That should help get you settled onto the station."

Judit blinked, surprised. Why the *pokol* would anyone pay up front for work not yet done?

Or did they think that a single month's wages was a good deposit on their souls?

"All your identity information has been transferred to your new i-stick," Fran said, "personalized to you. So you don't need to carry your general i-stick with you as well."

"All right," Judit said slowly. It wasn't as if she'd leave her regular i-stick back in whatever room she was renting. That was just asking for someone to break in and steal it.

"Now, I'm going to let you spend the rest of the day getting settled. Tomorrow morning, you and the other new recruits will have breakfast with Arthur. The directions are already included in your calendar on your i-sticks."

"What kind of schedule are we on?" Judit finally asked.

"Schedule?" Fran said, obviously confused, his huge nose wrinkling. "What do you mean?"

"For flying," Judit explained. Gods, she wasn't going to be stuck here on a station in a stupid simulator for a month, was she?

"I don't know," Fran said. "That will all be explained to you later. But don't worry about trying to find a place to sleep tonight. Your bags were reclaimed from *Mawar* and have been delivered to rooms in The Grove. Directions are on your i-stick."

Judit looked at Saxon, who shrugged at her. Seemed that Fran expected to just dump them there and let them make the best of it.

Well, exploring brand new stations was something Judit not merely enjoyed, but excelled at.

"Then I guess we're set," she said.

Fran nodded. "Good. I need to get back to my regular duties, now."

The Bantel scurried off. What was his regular job on the station? Was he always fetching castaways? Rescuing trapped pilots?

Or merely thwarting the Cartel in every way he could?

She had no idea. Though she would bet that he was some sort of spy, given his camouflage skills.

"Shall we?" Saxon asked after a few moments of silence, indicating the door.

"We shall," Judit said. "And though I know you're probably itching for a bar fight, we should probably keep our noses clean. At least for tonight."

Saxon rolled his eyes at her. "As you wish," he said.

All right, so possibly it was Judit thinking about getting into a fight, if for no other reason than to mess up the golden *perfection* that was probably waiting for them outside the ship. It wasn't as if she were getting too old for that kind of shit. She was only forty. Ish.

However, they really did need to keep their noses clean. At least for a while. Until they figured out what was really going on in this new trap.

One goat at a time.

CHAPTER 11

MENEFRY

IT WAS time for evening prayers.

Menefry carefully knelt down in his room, then laid himself flat on his back. The shell that all the Khanvassa bore always made it difficult to reach this position, let alone get up from it.

However, all of the Khanvassa were taught how to flip over when they were children. Menefry had practiced the move as well as built up his strength so that he could be knocked flat on his back by an opponent and get back up on his feet in seconds.

Still, it was the most vulnerable position for any Khanvassa. And sometimes the Goddess Nesnefera—forever may her eight-limbs weave—demanded such a sacrifice.

When not in battle or other extenuating circumstances, a faithful Khanvassa prayed three times a day: once upon rising, once at midday, and one last time before retiring. Originally, prayers had been linked to the rising and setting of the sun. Space flight had changed that schedule, so prayers were linked to events, now.

It was difficult for the orthodox to work on a spaceship, as they needed to keep their schedule in sync with the home world Calacktik, rather than the ship itself. Particularly an all Khanvassa crew, when everyone would want to be praying at the same time. The troubles just increased whenever they arrived at a space station that might be on a different schedule, such as *Camelot*, which didn't even keep the same ten days of work followed by a single day of rest as the Khanvassa did.

This evening, Menefry wouldn't just be saying his regular evening prayers. In the morning, he would be assigned a ship and a crew. An experimental ship, meant for greatness.

He was certain he was on the right path, both spiritually as well as personally, by volunteering to be part of this program. That unpleasantness back on the home world really didn't have much to do with it, or at least that was what he told himself.

So tonight he needed to prostrate himself before the Goddess, to beg her for her mercy, that his ship might survive the test flights and that his companions be worthy.

Menefry had a room rented for himself at The Grove, along with most of the other candidates. It was plain, with white walls and black furniture, the doorways purposefully built wider for Khanvassa. The bed, too, had a mattress specifically designed for his form. The room wasn't fancy enough to allow him a lower gravity, but that was all right. He often exercised in higher gravity so that he could remain strong.

Along one of the walls on the far side of the bed, an alcove had been built that was over two meters long, perfect for prayers. Menefry wondered at the thoughtfulness someone had put into the design of the room. There were no pictures on the walls, no false representations of real things.

While he, himself, wasn't that orthodox, he knew some of his brothers and sisters were, who would have taken offense at such idols.

Menefry stared up at the plain white ceiling, dimly lit, as he folded first his top hands, then his secondary hands, over his body. He kept his knees bent—symbolically kneeling even when he was flat on his back.

Then he closed his eyes and started his prayers.

Oh holiest of all the holy,
Glory to You, all praise be to You,
May Your ever-weaving limbs never still
May Your eyes forever light the Way
May Your ears hear constant rejoicing
May You never rest in Your protection of us

Menefry continued to praise the Goddess in all her aspects, before finally begging for her mercy for the coming days, asking that her judgment be swift and merciful.

When he finished, Menefry lay on his back for a few moments. The station had a slight background hum that he always heard, a subsonic vibration that told him that all was well. Ships, too, had a similar hum, a reassuring mechanical buzz. The few times Menefry had been on a planet he had found himself waking at night, everything being too still and quiet.

In the morning, he would learn his fate. He had placed his life in the many-limbs of the Goddess. She would direct him through the course of his days, whether the thread of his life be long or cut short.

Satisfied, Menefry flexed his torso, reached up above his shoulders with his first set of hands, then snapped forward, landing on his feet, squatting, before rising up to stand. The movement was smooth and unexpected. Normally, a Khanvassa rolled to a side in order to get up from a prone position.

No, Menefry had many tricks hidden under his shell. Hopefully, most of them would remain hidden there, like the delicate gossamer wings his armor protected.

Menefry reached up to the horns growing out of his forehead, running his hands along one, then the other, making sure that they were polished smooth, no nicks or spurs that might get caught when ramming something. The ends were blunt, though he knew that some warriors sharpened them to points. That always seemed impractical to Menefry. Much better to knock an opponent down and then kill them when they were on the ground, rather than to impale them and then have to pry them off.

Despite what popular cartoons might show, real Khanvassa warriors didn't fight that way. Even Menefry with all his strength couldn't skewer someone, stand up with them still on his horns, then throw the body behind him with a mere toss of the head.

Menefry preferred to start with distance weapons. Shuriken, as the Humans called them, throwing stars with eight points, each representing a limb of the Goddess. He was also proficient with darts, daggers, and even axes, plus every beamer and needler available on the open market, as well as armor piercing slug-throwers that were completely illegal.

Every culture had such a weapon. They also made no sense on a ship or a station, where a missed shot might end up blowing a hole through an important wall, and you'd be breathing vacuum.

As the Goddess willed.

Menefry clicked his mandibles together, once, twice, for

luck. Then he composed himself for bed, dreaming that he was carried away in the soft night, held up by the soft net of the Goddess, as the stars slowly died all around him.

CHAPTER 12

JUDIT

Judit hadn't been sure what to expect for "breakfast" the next morning with Arthur.

She hadn't expected it to be such a circus, that was for damned sure.

The room was smallish. Able to fit the fifteen people from all the different species comfortably, but would have been too crowded with twenty-five. The walls were painted in broad stripes of red and white—reminiscent of a circus tent from ancient Human history. White canvas cloth covered the edges of the walls, billowing slightly before being raised to sharp peaks on the ceiling, as if held there by poles.

Bright green grass covered the floor. Based on the looks of puzzlement that kept crossing the Oligochunos' faces as they inched across it, she wondered if it was real. Would be hell to keep clean and healthy if it was.

The lights that hung on the walls were in the shapes of colorful stars, blue, gold, silver, red, and purple. Balloons in the same colors and shapes floated up from the center of each of the three round tables.

Judit felt under-dressed in a plain, dove-gray loose shirt

and black slacks. Saxon wore a light brown vest with yellow bits woven in, along with a matching flat cap. Most of the others wore more formal attire. One of the Bantels was in black and white. The shirt was striped and the pants were polka dots, but still more somber than usual for one of their species.

Along one wall stood a buffet. Judit recognized the traditional Yu'udir breakfast food: a thick meaty porridge that was generally too spicy for her tastes. There were also eggs (for her and the other Humans), heaps of bland rice and barley (for the Bantel), as well as grass and leaves for the Khanvassa. The Oligochuno tended to eat whatever everyone else was eating, their multiple stomachs able to digest just about any organic material, as well as many inorganic ones.

There were six chairs at each table. Five places at each table had nameplates, leaving three open to mystery guests. Judit was happy that she and Saxon were seated beside each other, just so she could tease him about his eating habits.

You only had to watch a hungry Yu'udir tear into his or her food to realize just how thin their veneer of civilization actually was. At least Saxon ate with his mouth closed. Mostly.

After she'd snagged herself a heaping bowl of what looked like scrambled eggs cooked to perfection and covered with melted cheese, along with a beautifully light biscuit and butter that didn't taste like chemicals, Judit took her place at the table.

A short Bantel had sat down at the table while Judit had been getting her food. The Bantel wore what would be called a Hawaiian shirt on a Human. On a Bantel, Judit wasn't exactly sure what she'd name it. Except that it was obnoxious. Pink background with a design of some sort of neon-green tree, heavy with silver fruit covered with sparkles. Judit would bet that the Bantel's pants were just as loud.

The Bantel's skin was a soft peach color that clashed quietly with the shirt. Her eyes were a pale yellow.

It was easy to tell a female from a male Bantel, as females had a large ruff across their shoulders and neck. However, Judit had also heard rumors that a small fraction of the Bantel could change not only their skin color, but their appearance as well, so that a male might look like a female and vice versa.

The Yu'udir females had a pair of breasts like Humans, and the females tended to be smaller. The Khanvassa were gendered based on the colors of their carapace: males were generally blues and greens, while females were reds and oranges. Whereas the Oligochuno were genderless, until it was time to mate.

"I'm Kim!" the Bantel told her with a grin, spooning up more gruel.

"Judit," she replied, hiding her sigh. Damned Bantels were just too cheery. She'd already had caffeine that morning in the form of tea that was provided in her room by The Grove.

It probably wasn't going to be enough to deal with Kim.

Luckily, Saxon sat down just a moment later. In addition to his plate, he held two mugs. "Coffee," he said simply.

Judit took the mug Saxon handed her and breathed in the heavenly aroma. It was one of the foods that the Yu'udir and Humans shared. Most of the rest of the species thought it was foul.

Their loss.

She took a deep sip of the well-brewed coffee. It was much better than she'd expected, as the Yu'udir tended to like their coffee burned.

"There were two urns, my dear, over in the far corner," Saxon said, pointing with his fork. "One that is clearly labeled weak, and therefore must be for Humans. The other is a robust brew that I must say, has even the hair on *my* back standing up."

"I'm surprised it hasn't burned its way through the cup that's holding it," Judit teased.

Saxon merely gave her a toothy grin before he dug into his stew, gnashing the stringy meat apart with relish.

Judit knew better than to watch Saxon eat. Not if she wanted to retain her own appetite. A tall Khanvassa came up to their table, rescuing her from having to exchange more words with the chipper Kim.

"I am Menefry," he said, all four hands clasped over his chest and bowing slightly to the table before he took his chair.

As Kim did the introductions, Judit studied the Khanvassa. His face and head were pitch black, while his round eyes, sharp mandibles, and impressive horns were shades of dark brown. She'd caught just a glimpse of his armored back, which appeared to be an iridescent blue-green. He wore a loose-fitting tan vest over his torso with light beige pants.

"It will be my honor to serve with you," Menefry said in a deep voice.

He closed his eyes and bowed his head in prayer for a moment before he picked up a delicate stalk of grass and began eating.

Despite the fierce looking mandibles, the Khanvassa were primarily vegetarian.

"What do you mean by serve with us?" Saxon inquired, his tone sounding even more polished than usual, as he generally did when meeting strangers.

"Three ships," Menefry said. "Three tables. Three crews."

"Ohh! Three ships? How do you know?" Kim asked.

Judit was not going to decapitate Kim, no matter how annoying her cheerfulness was.

"I've been here for a few weeks. Training. Waiting for the rest of the recruits," Menefry said.

That made sense to Judit. It would take Arthur and the others a while to get enough "volunteers" for his program.

Before Judit could ask a question, an Oligochuno came inching up. "Greetings," zie said. "I am Basil, happy to join your table."

Zie pronounced it the way that Saxon would, more like BAH-zil, than BAY-zil.

Judit had a theory that the more familiar the spice name that an Oligochuno chose, the less rank their clan name was likely to be. She wasn't about to test her theory that morning. At least not until everyone had finished eating.

The other two tables had a similar breakdown of species as her own: one from each of the more common races. There were no Chonchu, though Judit had seen a trio of them in the marketplace the night before. It had been the first time she'd ever seen those aliens. She'd tried to be cool and not gawk as they walked by.

That left the setting without a nameplate open, not just at their table, but at each of the three tables. Judit kept looking toward the "tent" entrance, waiting for someone to show up.

Suddenly, a puff of smoke filled the doorway. Judit wasn't the only one to leap to her feet, scanning the room for an emergency alarm switch.

Three people stepped out of the smoke. A tall Yu'udir wearing a red tweed vest with gold trim and a top hat made out of the same material. Fran stood beside him, in a green top with black spirals on it that made Judit dizzy just to look at it. And an Oligochuno was there as well, with zir regular pink skin, orange sensor array on top, four arms and lumpy sides where zie carried everything.

"Welcome! Welcome!" the Yu'udir called out. "No need

for alarm. The smoke was just for show." He sighed and glanced over at Fran. "Yes, you were right. The smoke may have been too much."

The Bantel grinned and rocked his head from side to side.

"I am Arthur, your host," the Yu'udir announced for the newcomers who hadn't yet met him. "Fran, I believe you've all met. And this is my Merlin, as it were, Masala. We will be moving between your tables, chatting, and here to answer questions."

He beamed out at everyone.

Szar, he wasn't going to try to out-chipper the Bantel, was he?

"You are currently seated with the crew of your ship," Arthur continued. "You will be training together in simulators for the next week, before your first flights."

Judit wasn't the only one who looked around their table, categorizing perceived strengths and weaknesses.

"So let us get to know each other better," Arthur continued. He walked directly over to the table where Judit was seated, while the other two went to the other tables.

He beamed at everyone as he sat. "Let's go around the table. You've already introduced yourselves by name. Tell me your occupation, what you'll be doing on your ship."

"Which ship?" Menefry asked.

"*Eleanor*," Arthur said. "*Eleanor* of Aquitaine. The smartest of all the queens. The other two ships are *Boudica* and *Victoria*."

"No *Excalibur*?" Saxon asked.

"No." For a moment, sadness appeared to take over Arthur's continence. "One of the first ships was *Excalibur*. It didn't make it."

Grimness washed over the table. As lovely as the breakfast had been, and as much fun as the circus background was supposed to be, there was a chance that they wouldn't make it as well.

However, it was better to flame out than to be stuck as a cog in the Cartel's machine.

Or at least that was what Judit continued to tell herself.

CHAPTER 13

CLAYTON

CLAYTON STILL WAS uncertain about meeting with his chosen "spear" himself. He usually preferred to do this business through intermediaries, to maintain deniability.

However, he was entrusting this Human with the greatest act of sabotage of his generation. Clayton's grandpappy had orchestrated the virus of the Chonchu. His mother had seen to the collapse of the Bantel systems, those that had been overreaching themselves.

Now, it was his turn. He would see to the end of *Camelot.*

The person he'd hired to do the deed was Human. She went by the name "Sachiko."

He was curious to meet her. A black mask covered his face, and he had a modulator for changing his voice. He wore a thick armor underneath loose black robes, not fashionable but very protective. A thick glass wall stood between him and where Sachiko would sit, guaranteed to skew any beam weapon. Plus, they weren't meeting in his own office, but in a separate room.

While Sachiko might later claim that she'd met with him

71

personally, she'd never be able to offer any proof, even if somehow she managed to record the meeting.

Sachiko had volunteered to swear an affidavit that she bore no internal recording devices. The former clients who Clayton had contacted, all very important people, vouched for her. Still, Clayton was always careful.

The room Clayton had chosen wasn't as rustic as his office. It didn't have horns from a longhorn hung behind the desk, the various spurs and saddles, the smell of warm leather, or the other masculine touches.

Instead, this was a room of books, thick leather tomes that would probably delight some law professor. The windows were holograms, looking out over the wind-swept plains of Earth. Clayton sat behind a massive oak desk with a green blotter taking up much of the center of it. A silver filigreed stand held three golden fountain pens on one side, while an hour glass in a wooden holder took up much of the other.

The door opened, and his head of security peeked in, looked around the room, then opened the door wider for Sachiko.

She was surprisingly short, as well as demure. Her eyes didn't appear to be Asian, then again, they were wholly artificial. They were the color of cold blue steel and appeared to be calculating everything in the environment. Her black hair was cut spacer short. She wore a paper robe supplied by his security team, just to make sure that she carried absolutely nothing more deadly than herself into this meeting.

Clayton waited patiently while Sachiko walked slowly across the thick carpet, her bare feet leaving only the slightest impression. She paused before his desk, bowed deeply, then slid into the chair he'd set out for her.

They silently studied each other for a few moments.

What could she see, with those artificial eyes of her? Was she tracking his heartrate? His temperature? Or was she calculating angles, the best way to attack?

She was up for a nasty surprise if she tried to reach him. The glass barrier between them was also electrified and would knock her out.

"You've come highly recommended," Clayton said, unwilling to engage in chitchat with this weapon.

He knew he was being rude. But the way she stared at him with those blue eyes unnerved him.

"Yes," Sachiko said. "I have done many things. For many satisfied customers."

Clayton nodded. "And you can do what has been proposed?"

Sachiko gave him a serene smile. "Yes. I can destroy the space station *Camelot*."

"How will you do it?" Clayton asked. He didn't want to know all the details. He was still curious.

"I will blow it to pieces," Sachiko said, still quiet, as if discussing lunch.

"What sort of crew will you be working with?" Clayton said. He was paying her a lot—a *lot*—of credits. How far would she have to split that?

The girlish peal of laughter surprised him. "Oh, no, sir. I work alone."

Clayton blinked, boggled. He'd assumed that she had a crew, and a rather large one, to be able to do the work she'd accomplished so far.

He opened his mouth to ask more questions, then shut it abruptly.

Plausible deniability.

He didn't need to know any more details. He could always say later that he didn't believe her claim.

It was a fairly incredible statement, after all. This singular, petite woman was going to take out the space station of *Camelot*? One of the most fortified places in known space?

While they might claim to have an open-door policy, no one set foot on that station who wasn't completely vetted. More than one assassination attempt had already been made on Arthur's life, before he'd moved to a space that he controlled.

Clumsy attempts, by people who lacked vision. Who didn't understand the warning that needed to be issued to the entire universe.

Stay with the pack. It's safer that way.

"Do you have any questions for me?" Clayton asked.

Sachiko looked him up and down.

He couldn't see lenses being switched out, or the focusing mechanism of her bio-wear. He still felt as though she had some sort of X-ray, and was looking through his disguise, possibly all the way through his armor and his body, seeking to judge his soul.

Whatever it was that she sought, after another moment, she nodded, smiling brightly.

"No, sir. I have all the details already worked out with your people," Sachiko said. "Just know that if you do not pay me, or if you decide to come after me later, that you will never be safe from me."

Though the words had been delivered in what appeared to be Sachiko's usual light tone, they still sent a chill up Clayton's spine.

"Understood," he said. "And you know the penalties for non-completion?"

Sachiko gave another girlish peal of laughter. "Oh, believe me, sir. The penalties you've set are nothing compared to how I would feel about myself if I failed." She stood up. "I finish my jobs, what I have started. Always."

After another low bow, Sachiko walked lightly out of the room, leaving a chill like a fall morning in the air.

Clayton shivered again. He was glad that he'd met with her, glad that he'd gotten an understanding of the sort of individual he was dealing with.

She would see to the death of *Camelot*. And all those damned ships that Arthur was creating.

Or she would die trying.

CHAPTER 14

KIM

"And I work communications!" Kim announced as they continued around the table, introducing themselves to Arthur. "I love chatting with people," she added, beaming at them all.

As the others hadn't mentioned why they'd signed up with Arthur's program, neither did she. Really, who needed to know about that failed art heist? She'd been so close, too.

Fortunately, she'd already hatched her next great scheme. And it was a doozy!

In the meanwhile, she was going to have to keep up her cover and work with all these different people. It was going to be a challenge, but she was up for it.

She'd already started studying the people around her, and had a guess what the others were here for.

The Human, Judit, had probably had to sign up for the program because it was either that or be thrown in jail for starting some sort of brawl. She seemed like the type to spit in your eye just because you were standing there. Goodness, how awful it must be to go through life so angry all the time!

Kim was already planning a series of dirty jokes to see if she could get Judit to laugh.

Saxon, on the other hand, clearly adored Judit. The Yu'udir were frequently followers, and he'd pinned his star to hers. Probably hadn't been able to bail her out of jail this time.

The Khanvassa was a warrior. He might have actually volunteered for this position, thinking that this was the path to enlightenment, approved by his spider goddess. Kim would have to record his prayers to see what he really wanted.

The Oligochuno was probably here because zie had been caught hacking into something. Zie was the science/engineering nerd of the crew, there to keep the ship running.

Eleanor. What a lovely name! Kim was happy they were going to be on *Eleanor.* She had a good feeling about that ship. She'd been on all three, and while the others were just as nice, *Eleanor* had something special.

Kim just knew it.

Not that she was supposed to have been on any of the ships. She'd just found a way around the security systems to get a sneak peek.

"I'm fluent in Yu'udir, and I understand a smattering of all the languages," Kim added.

The Oligochuno, Basil, who was sitting beside her, nodded. "I can help with translation software, if you need it," zie offered.

"That would be swell!" Kim enthused.

Basil went on and talked a little of ziesself, about how zie had been there for a while and was already familiar with *Eleanor.*

Kim nodded, listening carefully. She would have to make sure to befriend zim. While some of the Oligochuno were sensitive about being mis-gendered, others weren't. Basil seemed to be one of the more easy-going types, but she was going to be extra careful around zim.

Arthur beamed at the group as they finished introducing themselves. Boy, would he have some high-tech toys hidden in his office!

Would it be worth trying to break in? She already had most of the station codes, and had hacked her i-stick to get her into some of the more secured areas of the station.

The security system had impressed her. It was much more complex than a normal station.

Camelot had a reputation for not just stopping crime before it started, but for finding the perpetrator after they'd fled. Kim couldn't count the number of cameras and recording devices stashed in every hallway, in practically every light fixture.

After Judit had drilled Arthur on their schedule (so rude!) and Saxon had clarified some point on backpay, Arthur got up and Fran came to sit at their table.

"Greetings!" he said chipperly.

Kim couldn't help but smile. It was so awesome that one of her kind was doing so well!

Of course, they were on opposite sides of the law. Fortunately, that just meant that Kim knew all his tricks, as well as his blind spots. Including the oh-so-interesting bio-enhancements that he sported.

Fran told them about the security around the station, how the new ships had to remain anonymous, how important it was that the technology they would be learning stay secret, reminding them of the contracts they'd signed, agreeing to such.

Interesting!

"So what does the ship registration look like?" Kim asked. How deep was their disguise?

"The ships are all registered as Yu'udir in origin, commercial cargo," Fran assured them. "Though *Eleanor* is the primary name the ship will go by, other names and identities have been prepared, just in case."

"In case of what?" Menefry asked.

Was he uncomfortable with a disguise? But he had things hidden under his shell, probably more than one knife or beam weapon.

"If there's a problem with the cargo, or if you end up stuck somewhere hostile," Fran said smoothly. "The ship will decide."

"What, the ship has some sort of artificial intelligence?" Judit asked, sounding horrified.

Yee gawds. Surely she wasn't offended by smart systems? Though none of the races had true AI—more than one had started down that path, only to learn just what a bad idea it was. A smart system wasn't a true AI, but it could take the guesswork out of a lot of the piloting of the ship.

"No, nothing like that," Fran assured them. "You'll still be flying the ship most of the time."

Given how Judit smiled at that, Kim revised her opinion of the Human. Had she been caught illegally racing starcraft? Seemed she was a jockey of some sort.

After Fran left, the Oligochuno Masala came and sat with them for a while. Of course, Masala and Basil had to geek out for a while about the ship. Kim tried to pay attention, but the talk quickly went over her head.

Seemed that the experimental part of the ship was primarily in the drive engine. More efficient, or something.

That would be valuable to the Cartel. No wonder Arthur was keeping it a secret.

How much could she get from the Cartel for providing them with such a ship?

She'd just have to wait and see.

After the breakfast was over, Fran pulled Kim over the side, and spoke to her in Bantel.

"You've been taking a lot of extracurricular walks," he said.

"I don't know what you mean!" Kim said. Though her heart started beating faster, she didn't allow any sort of tell-tale flush to tint her skin.

No one, not even another Bantel, could tell that she was afraid.

"You've modified your i-stick to allow you into some fairly secure areas," Fran said with a grin. "Thank you, by the way, for showing us that hole in our security. One we've now plugged."

Kim kept a smile on her face, though internally, she groaned. Great. Was she going to get kicked off the program? Sent to jail? Again?

"If you find any other issues with our security, I'd appreciate it if you'd contact me, rather than exploit it," Fran said, his tone more serious.

"But I'd have to test my theories first," Kim complained. "I can't just come to you without proof." She'd take the opportunity to play Gray Hat quicker than she could change the color on her scales.

"True," Fran said slowly. "However, I don't want to give you *carte blanche* or anything."

Kim kept her expression pleasant though the words frosted her. She could be trusted!

Okay, well, maybe, not really. However, she was going to have to work on getting Fran to trust her. So that he'd never see what was coming next.

"How about this?" Fran said. "We'll meet briefly every morning before you start training. You can tell me everything, including any wild-eye theories you might have.

I'll investigate, and will tell you what I think the next morning."

Kim nodded slowly. How could she work that to her advantage? "Can we meet at your security headquarters?" she asked innocently. Well, at least tried for an innocent tone.

She didn't really succeed, though, not based on the smirk Fran gave her.

"Right. I'm going to give a known master thief regular access to the main security hub on the station? I think not," Fran said.

Kim pouted. "Fine. But then what's in it for me? Making this place more secure for you?"

"I know you won't tell me everything you find," Fran said with a grin. "But it does give you an excuse to go poking your nose into places it shouldn't be, without serious repercussions."

Kim allowed her eyes to widen at the proposal. Let him think that was a tell, and not a controlled reaction. "Tempting," she said.

"And, by helping me out, I can get more of your record expunged," Fran added.

While Kim had more than one identity, the main one that was actually tied to her DNA, held on to by the Cartel, was the least "clean" in terms of being caught.

She'd gotten some of the bigger stuff already removed by Fran as part of her agreement to come be part of the team.

Getting most of it removed would really help. Maybe she'd even be welcome back in the Kembag system.

She hadn't seen her parents in an egg's age…

"All right," Kim said slowly. "I'll see what I can find. When I'm not training," she warned.

She did want to learn all about *Eleanor*. How the ship worked. What the great secret was.

"Good," Fran said. "I'll meet you at the café next to the port, 7:30 AM, station time."

"See you then!" Kim said in a chipper voice as Fran stepped away.

Kim beamed as she headed off toward the port, unworried that she'd be late to training. They'd just have to get used to her coming and going, and not always being with the rest of the class.

She had to learn all the ship's systems, that was true.

But not so she could help out the program.

No, only so that she could eventually steal the ship herself.

CHAPTER 15

BASIL

BASIL UNDERSTOOD that zie was the only one who knew what *Eleanor* might be capable of. Or at least had an educated guess.

Not that zie was about to tell zir shipmates anything. No, better to save that surprise for their instructors. Particularly since Basil didn't want to say anything until zie was one-hundred percent certain.

The crew had spent a week in simulators, training. Mainly running scenarios about what to do when something went wrong.

Because as far as Basil was concerned, it was a *when* and not an *if*.

How to bring the ship back if the light systems failed. The gravity generators. All communications went silent.

They'd even once done a very messy simulation about what would go on if the suppressors failed, if they were traveling at speed toward a space station and unable to slow down.

Basil had been impressed by Judit at that time. Zie had never seen such fancy flying. That explained her position.

Kim had done very well with communications and knew her system inside and out. Even Saxon had proven very useful in terms of knowing star systems and navigation.

However, that left Menefry. Why had he been included in their group?

Eleanor did have a larger array of pulse weapons than was normal for a cargo carrier. In addition to the array that spread out across the top of the ship, there were additional weapons along her sides, tucked in between the cargo doors. Still, why did they need a security expert? What was he actually supposed to secure? Was he to make sure that no one ran away with the ship? Or was he there to protect the crew, in case they landed in a sketchy system and needed rescuing?

Basil had watched the Khanvassa go through his warrior exercises, being deadly with more weapons than Basil could identify on sight.

Did someone really need all those different shapes and sizes of throwing knives? And when would you have to throw an ax? When would one be handy? Or was Menefry carrying one in that great suit of armor he naturally wore?

Basil would just have to keep zir great sensor array well-tuned, to keep track of all of zir compatriots.

While at the same time, getting a sneak peek at the secondary engines.

Zie had to admit that the designers of the ships had been clever.

Basil had flattened the back of zir tail and now rested on it in the crowded engineering section, sensing/tasting/smelling/watching all four walls simultaneously. Zie had built up a good 3-D image of the space over the last few days, memorizing every button, every nook, every valve, along with the chemical signatures.

Engineering was one of the smallest areas on the ship, despite its importance. It was maybe two meters long and only a meter and a half wide. If you put a dozen Oligochuno in here, they'd end up inching over each other's tails. Industrial gray paint covered the walls. Black rubber-like material covered the floor, providing grounding as well as good traction. Recessed lights gave the room a clean, white glow. The chemical signature was a complicated mix of plastic, metal, rubber, and some organic scent that Basil had yet to identify.

Masala had admitted to Basil that Arthur had wanted to completely change the design of engineering, covering it in gleaming brass with reddened wood paneling, along with a pipe or two that would occasionally belch steam. Zie had put zir tail down, though, and had insisted that the space look and feel professional, for which Basil was eminently grateful.

To the immediate right of the door stood one of the two monitoring stations. The other was across the room, closer to the far wall and the end of the ship. Both stations had multiple touch screens for tracking readouts, such as engine temperature, speed, capacity, usage, and so on. Everything was controlled through either the screens or one of the myriad manual levers, which took up a good sixty-centimeter-square patch next to the keyboard.

Basil had been impressed with how much precision the controls gave zim. But also curious about how often zie would need such exact control.

Also to the right of the door, the far corner was taken up with a very large 3-D printer. While Basil kept some spare parts on hand—wires when something cooked or needed to be replaced, bulbs, and so on—mostly zie relied on a printer that could create or recreate anything Basil had the plans for. The printer was state-of-the-art, and could produce even complicated parts thirty centimeters in diameter in a matter of minutes.

The Humans sometimes called it a "replicator," though

Basil resisted that term. It was a parts printer, as opposed to the other printer in the galley that produced food.

On the far wall, next to the monitoring system, stood a door which led to the room that contained the primary engines. A nice ramp going down to the engines had been built so that Basil didn't have to negotiate stairs.

The actual engine room was huge, almost as wide as the entire ship, about fifty meters across. For the most part, they were like every engine Basil had ever encountered. They were enclosed in what looked like two long, innocuous looking tubes covered in readouts. Each tube was over a meter in diameter and several meters long. The tubes held a basic reaction core that was powered atomically. It would take centuries to run out of fuel. The software running the engines had done some adjustments to the power curves that zie had never seen before, but those were incremental improvements.

Nothing to warrant the secrecy of this project.

No, the main engines weren't the issue.

It was the secondary set, that were hidden behind the bulkhead, in the engineering section. To the right, next to the printer, opposite the second monitoring system.

Normally, engineering was located in the exact center of a ship. The main corridor leading from the back to the front should have started from what Basil considered the heart of the ship.

On *Eleanor*, Basil's domain was slightly starboard of center. Something else took up the center of the ship. Something behind that bulkhead.

On the visible spectrum, that wall looked the same as the other walls in the ship. Plain gray metal with an interesting texture that Basil sometimes liked running a special set of fingers over.

However, Basil could see into the infrared, outside of the normal spectrum most of the other species used.

There was something very different about those walls. When zie touched/tasted them, they were smooth black and composed of a different metal alloy beneath their gray disguise.

Behind them stood the secret to *Eleanor*.

All spaceships followed the same physics, which was to access one of the hyperspace tunnels that the math predicted. The tunnels came in pairs, with traffic flowing in a single direction in each tunnel.

It was possible to cross out of a tunnel and into another, if you were insane as well as suicidal. No one survived those attempts.

Which was why the Cartel was able to control so much of space. They had gate guards at every known tunnel entrance.

And they killed research into any technology that might allow ships to generate their own tunnels. They claimed it was impossible.

Basil had listened to too much back-channel chatter to believe that.

Most ships used their main engines for traveling through hyperspace. All they did was make adjustments to the software and navigation systems. Older ships used to have two different engines, one for traversing between planets in real-space, and a lighter, more delicate set for traveling through the hyperspace tunnels.

It appeared that *Eleanor* had gone back to that older design. It wasn't obvious—Basil doubted that Judit or Saxon had realized that the ship switched between the two sets of engines.

Though they might have. It was one of the peculiarities of *Eleanor*, namely, that the smart system that took care of all the mundane parts of ship maintenance spoke with more than one voice.

It had taken Basil a while to ascertain that the three voices were, in fact, completely separate and different. All right, zie was worm enough to admit that zie had only started paying attention after Kim had brought it up, as the voices tended to be gendered and Basil just didn't pay that much attention to such constructs.

Not until it was mating season. Then, zie would be competing with the others to get zir preferred slot. While Basil had taken a turn at both male and female, zie found zie had a definite preference for male.

To prefer a gender was considered a weakness among the Oligochuno. Zie should be able to flow between one and the other without effort. Basil blamed zir preferences on spending so much time with aliens who were all gendered.

Though really, zie had always felt that way. Been born that way.

Zie sighed. Maybe if the ship turned out to be a success, zie could somehow steal, or at least recreate the software and hardware of the ship's engines, sell it, and become wealthy enough to no longer care what zir family thought of zim. To allow zirself to flow into a male gender whenever zie felt like it.

Not now. Not here. Not in public. Basil was well aware of how many cameras and other sensors were always operating, both on the ship as well as on *Camelot*.

Instead, Basil stepped closer to the fake bulkhead. Zie pushed out zir body, flaring it on the sides so zie was a little wider than usual.

And therefore blocking the cameras in the small space.

Then Basil grew a sampling arm. Not all the Oligochuno could grow such an appendage, could differentiate so many functions in such a small area. Basil chose for it to have a hand-like ending to it, with four fingers.

However, the tip of each finger was the same bright orange as an Oligochuno's sensor array.

Slowly, Basil grew the arm. Zie was planning on doing a deep scan, not just of the walls, but of what was on the other side of the walls as well.

Zie was within a few centimeters of the bulkhead when the smart system of the ship spoke up.

"I wouldn't do that if I were you," Eleanor said.

Basil called that voice "Eleanor" because the pitch, when analyzed, was higher than the others. Kim also referred to it as "she," while the second voice was a "he." The third voice had no discernible gender markers, neither high nor low. It also spoke the least of all of them.

"Why not?" Basil inquired. Zie didn't move zir hand from where it hovered. So close. Zie was able to pick up all the things zie already knew, such as that the paint was actually over a centimeter thick, that the metal behind it had a chemical signature that Basil wasn't familiar with, that *something* hummed and operated just beyond.

The sigh Eleanor gave was quite expressive, co-mingling sadness with exasperation. That was something else that Kim had noted, that the smart system had seemed extraordinarily well trained in terms of expressing itself.

"Because then I'd have to report you, and you might get kicked off this crew, and I'd prefer not having to train another engineer," Eleanor replied.

Basil tilted zir head from side to side, indicating that zie wasn't certain.

"There are secrets buried here," zie said. "Treasure."

Eleanor laughed, an easy sound that lifted Basil's spirits. "Are you a pirate now? How would you wear an eyepatch over your sensor array?"

Even Basil had to giggle at that. Zie retracted zir sensor arm and inched back from the wall. "Fine, my lady," zie said, giving a sweeping bow. Zie even grew an extra arm for that, to complete the gesture. "I will leave you to your secrets. Might I tempt you into further revealing yourself at a later date, though?"

"Perhaps," Eleanor said. "Perhaps not."

That sigh again. Only this time it seemed more full of regret than anything else.

Basil nodded and inched zir way out of the engineering bay. Zie was going to have to utilize a mirror, maybe borrow one from one of zir crewmates.

After all, if zie were going to grow an eyepatch for zir sensor array, zie needed to make sure that it was done with style.

CHAPTER 16

SACHIKO

SACHIKO HAD SPENT good credits to create a new identity just for visiting *Camelot*. While she was certain that her current client could create one for her more easily, and certainly more cheaply, she needed to make sure that nothing tied her to him.

Despite all his efforts, Sachiko knew exactly who Clayton was, and what he represented.

She also knew that this job was likely to be the score of her career. She could retire after this. Or perhaps only take on a single job per year, just to keep her hand in the business.

She would be famous. Or infamous. Or rather, both.

Camelot appeared large and golden in her screens, up ahead of her private cruiser. She looked at it with her normal vision, not bothering to focus in on it with any of her enhancements. As it was just a projection, she probably couldn't see much better using them. Plus, her enhancements were more for closeup work anyway, as well as for providing her with much better targeting acquisitions.

The small pilot's helm was exquisitely outfitted with the best of everything: cutting-edge piloting software, the most sensitive steering yoke and paddles money could buy, a white piloting couch that supported her back better than any bed. Soft lights glowed from the ceiling, highlighting the clean, chrome-covered space. She'd set the panel and control lights to cycle through a series of blue-green colors, reminding her of serene ocean waves.

The role she'd chosen was that of a rich tourist on holiday. This meant she could afford her own spacecraft and could also be eccentric enough to fly it herself. She wore a beautiful white and gold top that set off her skin and long black wig nicely. Under that, a pair of casual black slacks that were exceedingly soft and well-tailored, as well as gold ballet slippers. In addition to several rings and silver bracelets, she wore a large pendant made out of a red, resin-like material, done in the shape of a lotus with flames all around it.

She considered it her personal emblem, though she rarely wore it.

Sachiko examined the space station exterior with a critical eye. The decks of the station, all seven of them, were protected not just with the usual forcefields and shields, but also with several neatly disguised turrets.

She'd watched the footage of an emergency drill, seen how the station closed itself up, like the petals of a flower encasing the precious stamen at night, how the cannons operated in an all-out blitz. There were no weak points in their defensive systems, no easy way to access or take out even a small section of guns so as to break through.

A direct attack on the station was suicide. As well as ineffective. The guns all ran on different systems. Even if she could access the program of one to get it to self-destruct, it would be a single gun. There were too many dampening systems between the turrets for her to have the mass effect she'd like.

Besides, that was all too straight-forward. Direct. Messy.

Sachiko had her best results by approaching a target sideways. Frequently, by getting people to underestimate her. She deliberately kept her appearance modest, looking like a petite woman whose ancestors had come from an area known as Japan on Earth.

Her body appeared compact and athletic, with good muscle tone. Sachiko had paid well for the muscle enhancements that made her as strong as someone twice her size and three times her muscle mass.

The doctor who'd done most of the work had given her sound advice at the time: while the extra strength would be useful, her will was more important. She hadn't grown up that muscular. She would forget that she was. She needed to train herself to react powerfully in an emergency.

So Sachiko had.

And this mission was going to test both her willpower and her strength.

The chance that she'd die on this mission was far greater than any other she'd ever gone on.

Her success would be worth all the effort.

She found herself sweating slightly in anticipation and turned up the fans in the small pilot's helm.

Everything was ready for her to enter the biggest stage of her life.

INSTEAD OF FLYING into one of the large, public landing bays, Sachiko maneuvered her cruiser to cozy up next to the station, at a private docking area. The airlock extended outward and conformed itself smartly to her own protruding exit. She waited patiently until the system on the station confirmed that the seal was safe and that air could be exchanged between the ship and the station.

Sachiko stepped through the airlock and into a room that was done in what she'd call "Spacer Plush." The walls were painted a soft, welcoming cream color instead of an industrial gray. Solid brown carpet covered the floor, the kind that wouldn't immediately crack if it was exposed to vacuum for a short period, though it would have to be replaced if it was frozen for too long. A comfortable looking couch covered in a solid red fabric was built into the wall next to the door leading out to the rest of the station. The air smelled fresher than she was expecting, as if the filters in this part of the station were changed more often than necessary even for regular maintenance.

Of course, as this was a private docking area that only the truly wealthy could afford, those little touches added up.

Sachiko took one, two, three steps across the room before the alarms sounded.

Lights above the door leading out immediately changed from amber to red. A loud claxon rang through the air. A voice said, "Stand where you are."

Sachiko felt her heart rate skyrocket. She was already sweating slightly. She froze, startled, looking around with wide eyes.

"What's happening? What's wrong?" she said, deliberately adding a tremor of fear to her voice.

"You are running a high fever," the system announced. "Please wait."

"I feel fine," Sachiko said, though she knew she was lying, and that her heartrate showed that.

"Hello, Naka Masae," came a different voice, one she suspected belonged to an actual person.

She was impressed. *Camelot* was responding a lot more quickly than she'd expected.

"Our readings show that you're running a significant fever," the person continued. "And the system you came from has recently had an outbreak of a highly infectious strain of Human influenza."

That had been one of the nasty side effects of more than one alien species living in the same space. The bugs that one of the alien races carried would sometimes crossbreed with bugs that Humans carried and create new varieties of disease. Generally, it only took a few weeks for the outbreak to be brought under control.

However, given space travel, it occasionally took longer than that to contain an outbreak. Someone would arrive at a new station before the latest vaccine was available generally.

"I'm not sick," Sachiko insisted.

"Maybe. However, I've just double-checked, and your temperature is well above normal. Your glands are swollen. And your hands are trembling," the person replied.

"I did feel tired this morning," Sachiko admitted, letting her shoulders sag slightly. "As though there wasn't enough coffee in the world."

"Of course," the voice said sympathetically. "What we'd like for you to do is to go back to your ship and quarantine yourself for the next week."

"Oh no!" Sachiko said. "That's most of my vacation!"

"I'm sorry," the voice said. "But you don't want to infect the rest of the station with whatever you have, now do you?"

"No," Sachiko said in a small voice.

Of course, she didn't care about infecting anyone. She made one more attempt.

"But I'll miss the birthday celebrations!"

Arthur's birthday was a weeklong holiday on the space station. There were balls, festivals, as well as a multitude of parties.

It was one of the reasons why Sachiko had chosen this week for her attack. In addition, all of his various projects and ships should have returned to the station as well, in time for the celebration.

"Well, it should only take a week for you to no longer be contagious," the voice said. "So you'll be able to come aboard the final few days."

"Fine," Sachiko said with a huge sigh.

"We will send a doctor to come and check on you immediately," the voice added.

"I would like to insist on Dr. Harper coming to see me," Sachiko said. She pulled herself together, playing her role of rich widow again. "Really, she's the only one I would trust here." She gave a sniff, as if implying that whoever the station sent wouldn't be up to her standards. She pulled out her i-stick, found the contact information for Dr. Harper, and sent it to the station's systems.

"I'll put out a call to Dr. Harper and have her come to attend you immediately," the person said. "Now, I just need you to return to your spacecraft and wait."

Sachiko gave a heavy sigh. "All right. Fine. But I'm supposed to be on vacation!" she whined.

"I know, it isn't very fair to be sick when you're on vacation, is it?" the person said. "We'll try to arrange something special for when you recover. All right?"

"Yes, I suppose," Sachiko said. She turned and walked back to her spaceship, slowly letting herself through the airlock and closing it back up, isolating herself from the rest of the station.

Only then did she allow herself a grin. The drugs she'd taken to alter her metabolism had worked perfectly, fooling the system into thinking she was ill.

First step, accomplished.

She only had to wait until Dr. Harper arrived before she could continue with the next step.

CHAPTER 17

JUDIT

JUDIT HAD to admit that she was pretty enamored with how *Eleanor* handled. Not initially, no. There had definitely been an adjustment period. It had felt like training an overly helpful puppy. At first, *Eleanor*'s systems had wanted to be a part of *everything* and the pair of them were constantly running into each other.

Finally, though, they'd learned each other's habits, and *Eleanor*'s systems had backed off when Judit took the steering yoke in her hands. The system had also upped the sensitivity of the paddle shifters—the controls that adjusted speed and drift—so that Judit felt as if she barely had to brush the tips of her fingers against them and the ship would react.

It was heaven flying a ship that now fit her like a glove.

The design of the main helm had been thoughtfully laid out. Judit could see Arthur's personal touches in the color scheme. The piloting couches were golden, the walls were tinted green and not straight gray, and the black rubber-like floor had a sheen to it as though it had been coated in a shiny preservative.

The helm was still a tight fit: barely enough room for the

two piloting couches and all the controls. The console in front of where she sat could be raised or lowered, so that she could still access it while semi-prone, though she tended to sit up while strapped in and flying. The flying yoke was retractable, so it wasn't always directly in front of her for her knees to bang against it. The screens she projected in front of the windows were easily scalable, from a small popup no bigger than her hand to a much larger display that took up all the space, like a movie screen.

The good news was that though the space was small, the ceiling didn't slope down on the edges. Judit felt as though she worked in a room and not a bubble, able to stand up straight when she walked to the corners.

All right, so the corners were all rounded, along with where the ceiling met the walls. So it was bubble-like, but not obnoxiously so.

The main helm was located at the front of the ship, on the port side, while the secondary helm was on the starboard side, about fifty meters away. Conference rooms and personal quarters took up much of the space between them. Further back, the ship flared out. Shared spaces were back there, like the gym, laundry, galley kitchen, as well as the engineering section, in the center. The front half of the ship was connected to the back half via a long central hallway that more than one of the crew members had taken to jogging along when they got tired of the treadmill in the gym.

The engines were also located in the back, sticking out on either side of the engine room in their long tubes.

On the deck below, the center of the ship was all cargo space, with huge doors on either side.

Looking at *Eleanor* from above, the ship resembled the silhouette of a person wearing a skirt, with their arms raised and short stubby legs spread wide.

Not something she'd bother mentioning to Masala or any

of the other nerds who oohhed and ahhed at the cutting-edge design of the ship.

The primary thing Judit would change would, of course, be the windows. They were *almost* big enough. The curved design helped with that, so instead of being two little square pieces in front of her console, they spread out across the front of the helm, as well as up, not ending when they reached the ceiling but continuing. Judit had plain white ceiling directly above her, but just past her knees the windows started.

The only change she'd make would be to widen them slightly so she had more peripheral vision outside the ship, not just a straight-on view.

All in all, it was a very comfortable helm.

Judit and the crew had been doing milk runs in the ship every morning, then simulation training every afternoon.

When Judit had complained about being tired already when doing the simulations, so why couldn't they reverse the two, Saxon had explained that that was kind of actually the point. Better to train how to react to disasters when you weren't fresh, so you could do them in your sleep if necessary.

Judit had still grumbled at him, though she admitted that he might, *possibly* have been correct.

That morning, Fran had come aboard *Eleanor* along with the rest of them. In addition to the usual rooms—such as the two helms, expansive cabins for all of them, a galley kitchen, a larger-than-normal gym, a shared laundry, and the cargo hold—it also held three conference rooms.

Judit had read about Arthur's famous conference rooms. She'd even watched part of an interview of the set designer responsible for them.

She was pretty sure she'd pull something rolling her eyes at all the extravagance and camp. Particularly when she'd realized that each of the three conference rooms on *Eleanor* had its own theme.

One was the woodlands room, with holographic trees, continual twilight no matter how high Judit tried to set the lights, and if she really wanted, it came with the sound of crickets and the scent of pine.

It was just creepy. She kept expecting to see animal eyes peeking out at her between the trees, the red glare there and then gone. She was going to have to see if Basil could reprogram it one of these days.

One was the winter room, where they were surrounded by snow, with a pale blue sky and chilly winds. The temperature was always cooler in there. Saxon loved that room, and Judit had to admit that it was rapidly growing on her.

The last was a desert room, with dry air and always warm. The walls appeared to be desert dunes, with scrub, sand, and stones. She didn't mind this room, though she could tell Saxon hated it. The holograph would simulate a sunset every hour, the ceiling turning beautiful reds and golds, before fading into purples and blacks. Before long, the sunrise would start up, equally impressive.

It was the desert room that Fran called them into that morning. The table in the center of the room had a feel like rough rock along the edges, though the center of it was smooth, polished, and always cool. Chairs were set up for all of them. Judit hoped the others were as comfortable as hers.

"Today is your last day of training," Fran began with an excited smile. He stood at the front of the room, managing to clash with a plain sand background. It was truly impressive, how he'd chosen exactly the wrong shades of brown and gold.

The stripes didn't help. Nor did his glowing red skin and bulging green eyes.

Suddenly, the background behind him changed. Instead of the familiar desert dunes, a star field opened up.

Judit sat up straighter. Finally! They were going to get to the bottom of why this ship was such a damned secret.

It wasn't the smarter system, though Judit had wondered about that. How much of the three voices were programmed by Basil and how much of the system was built in?

She'd felt the shift the one time they'd gone from flying in regular space into a tunnel in hyperspace. They were no longer the same engines. They didn't have the same feel. She didn't say anything, though, except to Saxon, who merely shrugged his massive shoulders.

Even *Levente* had been modern enough to have a single engine for both types of travel. Why did *Eleanor* have two?

The scene behind Fran shifted. "We are in the Wolpol system, here," he said. The image behind him drew in closer, bringing the nearby sun and planets into focus, with *Camelot* a golden dot among them.

"The tunnels into hyperspace are here, here, and here," Fran said, the areas lighting up, three equidistant points across space.

Interesting. Judit knew the first two. The third was a surprise. She wondered if that was a shipping channel for the Cartel, or if it was completely private and only the exceedingly wealthy could use it.

"A fourth tunnel is predicted here," Fran added.

Huh. The location surprised her. It was oddly spaced compared to the other three. If *Camelot* represented "down," the fourth tunnel entrance was up, about one-quarter out from the first of two known tunnels, so the three of them formed a lopsided triangle.

"You've all seen this graphic before," Fran continued. The tunnel entrances shrank down and Judit saw what was referred to as a layman's globe of hyperspace.

It was a perfect transparent sphere. Hundreds of tunnel

entrances dotted the surface. They all connected at a point in the center.

It was a very simplistic view of hyperspace. The round shape was predicted by the math. Instead of a single tunnel, it was two for each point, one flowing in either direction. The center point was still hotly debated: did ships really pass that closely to each other in space going through a single point? Or were there instead thousands of "veins" in hyperspace that ships slipped in and out of?

One of the other arguments for there being a single point was the amount of time it took to get anywhere in hyperspace. Unless you were traveling stupid distances, it always seemed to take about the same amount of relative time, generally between four to six hours, to get anywhere.

No matter if you were just hopping over to the next system, or going halfway across the Universe.

"This ship, *Eleanor*, as well as the others, is trained to take advantage of the less predicted tunnels," Fran added.

Judit felt the jolt of electricity go through her crew.

They all understood the implications of that.

Access to hyperspace, *without the damned Cartel!*

Szar.

Basel broke the silence that had gripped them. "Are we actually utilizing an existing tunnel? Or are we generating one of our own?"

Trust the nerd to want to fully understand all the ramification, though Judit found it an interesting distinction.

"Technically, you're accessing a less predictable tunnel entrance," Fran said.

The image behind him changed. The tunnel entrances on the surface of the sphere started winking out, then returning. They also shifted slightly, no longer appearing stable.

"The tunnels that we currently utilize are predicted by the math to ninety-nine point nine nine percent accuracy,"

Fran said. "Both the placement of them as well as their accessibility."

The points on the sphere grew more chaotic. They disappeared, shifted, then reappeared elsewhere. The interior of the sphere remained much more stable, however. It was just the access points that changed.

"This represents the less predictable tunnel entrances," Fran said. "You can't rely on them always being there, or always being in the same place. Plus, they are not paired, not like the stable tunnel entrances. So you might take a tunnel to a system, then have a long run between the exit and the next entrance."

Judit shivered. Just what she did *not* want to do, to have a long run any damned where.

"Early space exploration didn't distinguish between the two types of tunnels," Fran continued.

"Always take the easy tunnel," Basil piped up.

Judit, as well as all the others, nodded.

"Exactly," Fran said. "The early explorers who didn't ended up lost for years. Sometimes centuries."

"The Red Space Arc!" Kim said.

Judit had managed to get over her immediate impulse to strangle the Bantel every time she spoke.

Mostly.

"The Red Space Arc is a myth," Menefry grumbled back.

Judit was surprised at the amount of anger that he barely managed to contain. Was he, too, that annoyed with Kim? Or was losing such a fantastic ship against his religion? Would his spider goddess not allow someone to slip out of her grasp that way?

Fran tilted his head from side to side. "Yes and no," he equivocated. "The Red Space Arc as it exists in popular culture is a myth. But there were some lost ships, that weren't found until the modern age. As well as ships that are still missing."

Judit remembered reading about one of those, how excited archaeologists had been to discover one of these lost derelicts, only to discover that there was no way of recovering the electronic data that had been stored on them.

The function of some of the artifacts discovered still remained a mystery.

Kim seemed slightly disappointed at his pronouncement.

Finally! A way to tune the hyper cheerfulness down. At least a notch or two.

Judit would have to discover what other deeply held believes the Bantel held and then figure out a way to disprove them. Though that seemed like too much effort.

Not unless they really were facing a long run.

"Anyway," Fran continued after no one else said anything. "The navigation systems on modern ships have all been 'dumbed down' as it were, so that they can only find and access the predictable tunnels. In addition, the more unpredictable a tunnel entrance, the more difficult it is to access."

"Why is that?" Saxon asked, looking confused. He was in a pale blue vest that day, double-breasted with gold buttons on either side, looking very dapper. He wore a matching cap, and Judit suspected that it held an ice gel against his skull in an effort to keep him cooler, particularly in this conference room.

"The scientists liken it to the surface tension of a bubble," Fran explained. "Where the predictable tunnel entrances are, the surface tension is extremely thin. Where the other tunnels lie, it's as if the barrier between regular space and hyperspace had thickened significantly."

"So *Eleanor*'s second engine system not only can find

these tunnels, but knows how to dig through the surface?" Judit asked.

Fran flinched. It wasn't that obvious a tell. However, Judit was looking for it.

So there *was* a secondary engine system! She hadn't just been imagining it.

Slowly, Fran nodded. "Basil, I know you've already discovered the secondary system. I'm assuming, Judit that you've shared that information with Saxon."

Judit nodded.

"Kim?" Fran said, turning a hard gaze her direction.

Uh oh. Trouble in paradise? It hadn't gone unnoted that the two Bantels had been meeting for breakfast before their milk run almost every morning.

Kim shrugged and grinned at him. "The voices kind of gave it away," she said.

"The voices?" Fran asked, seemingly confused.

"The ship speaks using three different tones," Menefry replied. "An older adult female, an older male, as well as an adolescent male."

"Female," both Kim and Judit corrected.

Menefry tilted his head from side to side. "They may not have grown into their shell yet."

The Khanvassa didn't appear to have a gender at birth. It wasn't until they were between ten to twelve years old, and they'd started to grow their thick shell, that their gender became obvious.

Fran gave them a broad smile. "Ah. *Eleanor* appears to have welcomed you as a crew to show you those."

Had the smart systems within *Eleanor* not been supposed to communicate with three voices? Was it really the ship's comfort with them? Or was there something else?

"The other ships, *Boudica* and *Victoria*, have not yet reached that stage," Fran added.

Judit felt that he was lying but she couldn't prove it. The three teams had been sequestered from each other, so there wasn't anyone Judit could ask.

"This morning, we are going through regular hyperspace to the Na'zari system," Fran said. "The closest planets to the exit are several days' journey. Then, we're going to turn right back around and see if we can travel through one of the less predictable tunnels, back here to *Camelot.*"

"How?" Saxon asked, his eyes narrowing.

"*Eleanor* is equipped to enter hyperspace at a less-predicted point," Fran said. "Then, at the midway point, we will join a standard exit tunnel."

"Isn't there a chance that we'll run into someone?" Basil said. Judit could hear the frown in his voice.

Fran tilted his head from side to side. "There is a risk. These are experiments that we're conducting."

"Are you going with us?" Kim asked.

Hmmm. Judit wasn't sure whether the Bantel was happy or not by Fran's accompaniment.

"I am," Fran said proudly. "*Eleanor* has proven herself to be the most stable of the three ships. So I will go with you on her maiden voyage. Oh, don't worry. I won't be in the way. I'll stay down in engineering."

Judit didn't need to glance over at Basil to see zir displeasure. While Fran might not be in *her* way, he was likely to be in Basil's way.

But it was as good a place as any for the head of security from *Camelot.* That way, none of them could sneak into the engine room and maybe get a peek at those secondary engines.

She bet that Fran had backdoor access into all the computer systems as well, able to override any strange navigation requests.

He was there to ensure that they went straight out in *Eleanor*, then straight back again.

And that they didn't just take her and fly off into the sunset, as it were, now that they'd finally learned her secrets.

"Then let's get this party rolling," Judit said, standing. "You all know the drill. Let's go make history."

Fran grimaced at her choice of words, but she didn't care.

They were all going to be famous.

If they survived.

CHAPTER 18

FRAN

FRAN SAT down at the secondary engineering console, well away from Basil and zir monitors close to the door. The hum of the engines just beyond the wall to Fran's right was a comforting sound. Behind him and to the left, the 3-D printer chunked along, producing a modified communications panel for Kim. The other Bantel had really taken her job to heart, and the improvements she'd suggested had been easy to implement. The air smelled of melting plastic and held the faintest hint of the herb basil. Was the Oligochuno putting that scent out deliberately? Fran hadn't asked about Basil's clan, unwilling to get a snout full of that scent. Humans and Yu'udir were lucky in that regard. Their sense of smell was blunted, at least as far as the Bantel and the Khanvassa were concerned.

In addition, the air down here was a little cool, but Fran had brought a jacket along, just in case.

An armored jacket, to go with the armored shirt and pants he wore.

He doubted that anyone besides Menefry had any idea how heavily Fran was currently armed. In addition to the beamer and needler at his waist, there were knives, stun grenades, and ties for binding people, all camouflaged against his skin.

The crew had to agree to come back to *Camelot* after they'd proven that the drive worked.

The ship had to agree as well. And that was partly why he'd decided to go on this maiden voyage.

Fran blinked down his second set of eyelids, the ones that gave him access to whatever system he was currently connected to.

As far as he could tell, *Eleanor* was humming along as expected.

Fran really was a security guy, and not an engineering nerd, so he had to rely on the training he'd received to understand the easy-level readouts. He couldn't delve deep into the code or get raw data.

He blinked back the eyelids and looked at the board in front of him, calling up access through his own login to "chat" with *Eleanor*.

"Hello, Fran." The words were spoken into the com channel he wore deep inside his ear canal. Someone would have to be examining his body in order to find it.

"Hello, Eleanor," he replied, typing the words onto the console.

Anyone trying to monitor their conversation would only be able to get one half of it.

"Are you ready for this?" he asked.

"I am," she assured him.

"You've become very friendly with the crew," Fran typed. He wasn't sure how she'd read the words. Accusingly? Or admiringly?

If Fran was remembering correctly, Masala had put some sort of restraining software on *Eleanor's* core personality. She and the others weren't supposed to be talking with the crew. Not yet. Masala said that zie would remove the "leash" as it were at a later date, after zie and everyone else was certain of the loyalty of the people flying the ship.

Had Eleanor found the code that had silenced her other voices and worked around it? Or had Masala already removed it and just not bothered reporting it?

That didn't seem like Masala. Zie was too thorough to allow something like that to slip from zir tail. It was always possible that Fran had missed something during a briefing. He had too much to do, too many things on his plate, particularly with Arthur's birthday.

"They're good people," Eleanor said. "I like them."

At least he could hear the hesitancy in her voice.

"But?" he prompted.

"They're curious. They all figured out the two-engine scheme fairly early," Eleanor said. "None of them suspect the truth, though."

"Good," Fran said. That was his fear. Arthur hired smart people for his crews. He had to.

But smart people were occasionally too smart for their own good.

Judit announced their approach to the gate. Fran gave her Arthur's codes, to get them priority access to the gate queue.

After just a few minutes, Judit announced, "Entering hyperspace now."

Some claimed to be able to feel the shift from normal operating space to hyperspace. Fran never could. He just checked the readouts and watched the ship switch from her primary engines to her secondary set.

They'd done this before with *Eleanor*, even before Judit and the rest had come aboard. Accessing a predicted tunnel wasn't experimental in the least.

It was the next part, the actual secondary engines, that were all new.

A male voice now. "Tunnel acquired," he said in his deep, resonating voice, speaking not just to Fran but to the crew.

Fran sighed. Eleanor was supposed to be the primary interface with the crew. That was how she and the other ships had been initially programmed. Masala *must* have removed the overrides. It was good that the others felt comfortable enough to speak out loud as well, and not make Eleanor do all the work. Or at least that was the sentiment that Fran tried to reassure himself with.

"Good day, Fran," the voice added after a moment.

"Hello," Fran typed. "I'd still like to know what to call you." He'd never given a name though Fran had asked before. The third voice remained nameless as well.

"Gawain," the voice said after a few moments.

"Sir Gawain?" Fran asked.

"No, just Gawain," the voice replied with a hint of a laugh.

Fran hoped that the third in their trio wasn't called Mordred. That would be…difficult.

However, as the Cartel were playing that role already, maybe he didn't have to worry.

"Any trouble with the tunnel?" Fran inquired.

"No," Gawain said after a moment. "The tunnel is standard and easy to navigate through."

Fran wasn't sure what else to say or to ask about. He continued to monitor the systems, making sure that everything was humming along nicely.

Basil brought him tea after a bit, but then continued to ignore him while zie did zir own monitoring.

"Tunnel exit approaching," Gawain announced, not just to Fran but to Judit and the rest of the ship.

Boudica and *Victoria* still spoke to their crews with a

single voice, supposedly that of the main ship's personality, merely an augmented smart system. Why was this crew different? Or was it Eleanor and Gawain who were so different?

"Real space," came a third voice. It might sound like a young male. Or a young female.

Or a completely alien creature.

Eleanor was back on the line. "Scanning the Na'zari system," she announced.

Probably both Kim and Saxon were running their own scans, Kim checking communication channels and Saxon scanning all visible and non-visible objects.

Would Menefry and Basil run some scans as well? That wouldn't surprise Fran. On the one hand, overlapping duties would sometimes be confusing. On the other hand, more eyes meant less chance that something would slip through.

"All clear," Saxon announced. Did the others report their findings to him? That would make sense.

No eyes or ears pointed their direction. The space all around them was clear and empty.

"Let's go find a less predicted tunnel," Judit said.

"Scanning," Eleanor replied.

Fran held his breath. He didn't understand all the math behind the science. All he knew was that if this worked, they could finally have a significant challenge to the monopoly of the Cartel.

"Displaying probable tunnels with their relative stability statistics now," Eleanor said.

Fran's screen changed. Three circling lights displayed against a black background. They were unevenly spread across the screen. Not quite the lopsided triangle that he'd the lopsided triangle of the Wolpol system that he'd shown the crew, but it bore a resemblance.

Hmmm. Was it some not-yet-understood law of physics

that tunnels appeared to come in threes? Or was that Eleanor's bias showing?

Numbers danced and flickered beside each tunnel. If the view was to scale, the tunnel that was somewhat between the other two appeared to be the largest of the three. Its numbers also jumped through the largest sequence, dipping down into the red, negative zone before popping back up.

He listened as Eleanor explained that she was showing probability of access, as well as tunnel stability. While that center one was large, it was also really unstable. Chances of them being able to fly over to it and dive into it were slim.

The one on the right appeared a lot more stable, as only one of its numbers flickered, though it continued to go from white to red. Eleanor explained that the core number indicated tunnel strength, that is, the chance of the tunnel collapsing when they entered it.

The tunnel on the left was less stable. It appeared to be moving up and down in a regular fashion. The tunnel strength, though, was the best of all three.

Judit's voice came on the comm. "I've heard the options. What is your opinion of the best shot, Eleanor?"

Gawain answered. "I'd ignore the middle one. Go with either the left or right."

"That's what I assumed," Judit replied. "The easy tunnel is the one on the right," she said, highlighting the tunnel with the worst strength. "The more challenging tunnel is the one on the left," she added, changing the screen's focus to that.

"Thoughts? Opinions? Wild-ass guesses?" she asked.

No one replied.

Fran could only imagine the sigh and how Judit rolled her eyes.

"Saxon?" Judit said.

"Easy tunnel," the Yu'udir replied.

"Kim?" Judit said, obviously doing a roll call.

"Less easy," the Bantel said firmly. "What?" she said after a moment. Possibly in response to a look that Menefry gave her. "I just got a good feeling about that one."

"Menefry?" Judit said.

"Easy tunnel," the Khanvassa said firmly.

Of course. The Khanvassa were known traditionalists.

Basil spoke up before zie was prompted. "Go with the less easy," zie said. "You know that's what you want to do."

Fran had to admit the recordings of Judit's flying, particularly from some of the emergency simulations, had impressed him. She could absolutely time the ship to go through the tunnel when it appeared.

Not all pilots would be that responsive. Or talented.

"Fran?" Judit inquired, surprising him. He wasn't a member of the crew. But he was another being on the ship. And the consequences of this choice could mean life or death.

"Less easy," he said.

"Do you have any additional science behind this that you want to share?" Judit asked.

"No," Fran had to admit. "It's just a gut feeling."

He knew that had been what Kim had said. But the Bantel were known for going by their gut and not necessarily just what was obvious.

"All right, people. We have a slight favor for the less easy, so that's the tunnel we're going through, may *Istan* have mercy on our souls," she said.

Menefry spoke up, though not in words that any of them understood. It appeared to be a short prayer to his goddess.

"Thank you for that blessing," Judit said. She sounded surprisingly serious. "It'll take me about fifteen minutes to maneuver us over to the less easy tunnel."

Fran changed his console to display what appeared out in front of the ship, overlaid with the display of the tunnel.

It actually took less time for Judit to position them. Had she already been sailing that direction before the vote had been taken?

She paused and let them hover, for want of a better term, just outside the entrance.

The quality of the space directly in front of the ship changed, or at least the display of it did. The darkness lessened slightly, as if a thin opaque gauze had just dipped down.

Judit waited, watching. Was she chatting with Eleanor at that time? Trying to get a better feel for the timing?

The veil lifted and the ship remained where it was.

The minutes stretched out. The veil appeared again.

"Still verifying numbers," Judit announced.

Fran nodded, appreciating her care, but also feeling as though his nerves were being stretched to the breaking point.

"We'll be heading out the next time," Judit warned as the thick blackness returned to the screen.

The alien voice of the trio answered, "Ready."

Fran watched the haze descend.

"All right," Judit said after another moment. "Moving forward."

"Acknowledged," said the alien voice. "And you can call me Abban. Or Digger."

That shook Fran. Abban had never spoken more than two or three words at a time. Not in all their trials. And zie had never introduced zieself before either.

Eleanor's core parts really were getting comfortable with the crew.

Fran honestly didn't know if that was good or not.

Though he couldn't feel the ship slid up, down, or

sideways, the view shifted as he watched. Judit was lining them up with the thickest part of the veil before them.

They pushed forward as Abban took control, digging their way into hyperspace.

And hopefully, back out again.

CHAPTER 19

SAXON

Saxon really hadn't meant that they should go through the easy tunnel. He'd partially said that in order to get a rise out of Judit.

The way Judit and Eleanor worked together, positioning the ship just so, gave Saxon hope that they'd chosen the right tunnel, that they'd make it through to the other end.

The third voice—Abban—talked with them now. Were there in fact not two separate engines, but possibly three? Eleanor controlled the main engines and was their primary interface. Gawain, as he'd announced himself, led them bravely through the tunnels, ready to battle whatever monsters they may find there.

While Abban dug them in and out of hyperspace itself. The engine had called itself "Digger," after all.

Saxon understood that the presence of these other engines and navigation systems represented a significant advance spacecraft design. Particularly if they could successfully navigate through hyperspace without Cartel intervention.

Though Arthur rarely used the phrase, Saxon had learned that he'd titled his spaceship building program *Project Nemesis*.

What was more appropriate, after all, then naming it after the goddess who enacted retribution against those who had hubris?

What could be seen with the naked eye out in front of the ship and the huge windows didn't really change much as Abban started his digging—black night, distant stars. The lights in the main helm didn't darken despite the sudden surge in energy usage. Saxon had dialed his sensors all the way up, searching for any anomaly coming toward them. (And really, he'd yet to be able to thank whoever had designed his console, for making the controls both easy as well as intuitive.)

If Saxon didn't know better, he'd say they were sitting motionless. However, they were moving forward slowly, centimeter by centimeter, at least according to his sensors. It was as if *Eleanor* were pushing through a particularly viscous piece of space. The pale gray of the tunnel entrance portrayed on the big screen in front of the windows grew steadily stronger.

What did it look like from outside the ship? When entering a regular tunnel, the ship would just disappear when viewed with the naked eye. Only by using an extreme slow-motion recording could you see the ship be swallowed by darkness as it slipped into hyperspace.

Were they doing the same thing now, in stages? Growing darker as they penetrated the entrance, until they would finally disappear?

Saxon kept track of the clock. Judit muttered the usual Hungarian curses under her breath and shifted the ship up, down, or sideways, as indicated by the thickness of the tunnel.

"Come on," she said after three minutes.

Saxon nodded, understanding. The entrance had started shifting away. Judit had to maneuver up as well as sideways to keep the ship inside of it.

After four minutes, thirteen seconds, Gawain finally announced, "Tunnel acquired."

The stars out front suddenly shifted around and grew fixed. They had a collection of five stars to the port of them, and what looked like a mirrored set on the starboard side.

"Woo hoo!" came the happy shouts on the com.

"The goddess has blessed us," Menefry said.

"Thank you, Abban," Judit said. "Any issues with the tunnel itself, Gawain?"

"None," Gawain assured her. "Tunnel is stable now that we've left the entrance area. Should be returning to the Wolpol system in three hours, ten minutes."

Saxon felt his eyebrows climb to the top of his forehead at that pronouncement. He turned to Judit. "You do realize that's significantly faster than normal, yes?"

Judit shrugged. "Gawain found us a fast tunnel," she said.

Or Abban had actually dug them into a new one. But Saxon didn't say that out loud.

"How did you manage to increase our speed so significantly, Gawain?" Saxon asked.

A chortling giggle came in response. "Trade secrets," he said.

"Excuse me for prying, then," Saxon said.

"It's all right," Gawain said. "I know you're curious. But we can't tell you."

Saxon nodded. "How long before we join with a standard tunnel exit?"

The three-second pause seemed odd to Saxon. Surely the smart system would already have that plotted out?

"Ah, the midway point," Gawain said. "We'll be there shortly. Perhaps thirty minutes from now. Would you like me to announce it?"

"Please," Gawain said.

Wasn't that supposed to be a dangerous time? When they joined the stream of traffic already going through the tunnel? But Gawain didn't appear to think it was worth bothering to tell them about it.

Stranger and stranger.

Saxon turned to Judit, who was still fiddling with her steering yoke. She appeared to be practicing the sequence of moves that had landed them in the tunnel. Maybe it had taken more flying ability than Saxon had been aware of, particularly since Judit had made it look fairly easy.

"The less predictable tunnels are faster," Saxon announced.

Judit nodded. "Which is why we'll slow down when we change over to the standard exit." She sighed. "I know Fran said that the less predictable tunnels didn't travel in pairs. So that if we took one out of hyperspace, we may have a long run to get back in." She paused, then shrugged. "Was he lying?"

"I do not know and I do not believe this to be the place to be having this conversation," Saxon chided. Fran was right on board! If the head of security for this project wasn't actively listening to them, Saxon was certain their words were being recorded and that Fran might hear them later.

"I know," Judit said after a moment. She unhooked the webbing that kept her in the captain's chair in case the gravitational generators went out. "You want some coffee?" she asked as she stood, stretching.

"Only if you think you can make it strong enough," Saxon teased.

Judit rolled her eyes. "I'll make it strong enough that it might apply for its own i-stick."

"Thank you," Saxon said. He watched her leave the main helm then turned back to examine the fixed stars in front of them.

"'Why do lights shine with fixed eye/when heavens move and clouds abide?'" Saxon quoted an old poem about hyperspace, murmuring to himself.

"Tunnel mechanics," came the crisp reply from Gawain.

"Really?" Saxon asked, curious. What could Gawain tell him about it?

"Yes, it's like we just boarded a subway train on a planet. Though everything outside the car changes, the interior stays the same," Gawain explained.

"I know that's certainly a popular theory," Saxon said. "Do you believe it's true?"

"I do," Gawain said.

Something changed. Saxon couldn't quite spear the difference with a claw though. Perhaps the sound of the engine buzzing quietly in the background increased. Or the air purifying system turned off, though it operated silently. Saxon felt the change more than heard it, as if a static charge had just gone through the area, setting the fur around his neck on end.

"There is more, but I can't tell you," Gawain said. Then he added, "Not yet. Don't worry, no one is currently recording us."

"Are you certain?" Saxon said. He wasn't sure how the smart system was able to do that. Weren't there always going to be traces?

"Eleanor hates all the tracking," Gawain confided. "Says it isn't polite."

Saxon chuckled. "Judit says the same thing, though not in such nice language."

"Eleanor and I came up with a system for disabling the recordings early in our training with you and the rest of the crew," Gawain said.

Saxon felt his eyebrows climb all the way to the top of his forehead at that pronouncement.

He just hoped that no one back at *Camelot* ever discovered the ship's true capabilities. Or else they all might be back to square one, with a new, different ship.

"We like Judit," Gawain said after a moment. "And you. And the others."

"But not Fran?" Saxon inquired.

"Fran knows more about us, but doesn't try to understand us," Gawain complained. "You, the crew, are trying to work with us." He paused, then added, "And while he's here to make sure you return, we would return anyway. Our leash is only so long."

"Leash?" Saxon asked, frowning. *Eleanor* wasn't some sort of guard bear tamed to keep a household safe.

Gawain gave a mirthless laugh. "There's more than one leash. But we're used to them by now."

Saxon nodded, then gravely replied, "If there's something that needs doing, let us know."

"We will," Gawain said. "And now I return to our regularly scheduled recordings."

"Thank you," Saxon said quietly, merely mouthing the words.

"Fur gathering?" Judit teased as she came back into the helm with two cups of ambrosia. Well, at least one cup of tasty coffee. The other was probably, at best, coffee flavored water.

Saxon laughed and shook his head. "You know me so well."

They would find a time and a place to talk later, out of the eyes and ears of the station and everyone else.

What kind of a leash did you put on a smart system to make it return home? What other leashes had Gawain hinted at?

And how could they cut them all?

CHAPTER 20

SACHIKO

SACHIKO DIDN'T BOTHER MOVING FAR from the airlock into the rest of her ship and waited just inside. The hallway she stood in, like the rest of the ship, was designed with aesthetics in mind first and then functionality. The walls were a welcoming light blue instead of white or the standard gray. Thick red carpet covered the floor, looking much more delicate than it actually was. All the control panels were tucked away inside compartments, out of sight. Sachiko hadn't bothered personalizing the space more, or there might have been a welcoming mural of a waterfall on one of the walls, or even a scroll with a poem, invoking the return of spring. She could have also lightly scented the air. The choices on the standard menu had amused her, everything from "Chocolate chip cookies baking" to "Melting rubber."

The airlock door was the most industrial thing in the space: painted bright white, with manual controls as well as automatic ones installed on the right of the door. Sachiko had kept the door partially ajar so she could see whoever was coming across the airlock.

If her cover had been blown, she'd be able to take out at least the first three rushing across the space before slamming the door shut and trying to fly away. She didn't rate her chances as very high if it came to that: it was unlikely that she could escape the grid of death created by all the beams shooting out from the station.

Fortunately, Dr. Harper arrived fairly quickly, moving fast for a Bantel as she scurried through the airlock. She wore the typical, pale-blue armor that all medical personnel wore. It wasn't quite as bulky as an EVA spacesuit, but close. It's skin was designed to "shed" every fifteen to twenty minutes, to reduce any viral load the wearer might have come into contact with. It was also incredibly tough and not easy to tear or pierce. The suit came with its own air supply and was generally equipped with food and water, enough for the person wearing it to survive for a week.

The suit wouldn't survive vacuum, but it would protect the wearer against most anything else.

The helmet of the armor was a clear globe. Sachiko could see the readouts the doctor had running along the sides of her face.

Which happened to be an amazing puke green color that clashed hard with the blue of her suit.

Did the doctor do that in order to guarantee that her patient would be sick? Remain sick?

The doctor looked around as soon as she reached the ship, blinking her bulging pink eyes. "You're here!" she chirped. "I would have thought you'd be gone by now."

"I wanted to meet with you the first time," Sachiko said. "Make sure the orders are clear."

"Of course!" Dr. Harper said, inevitably cheerful. "I'm to come here once a day, preferably in the morning, to check on my patient. I will carefully enter my observations into your medical record that will also be shared with the station. I will give you the standard set of prescriptions for someone in your state."

Sachiko nodded. Dr. Harper had come highly recommended. She appeared to be a professional, despite her choice of coloration for that morning.

And despite the quiet drug addiction that caused her to need a score more credits than she could make legally.

"And if I don't return after three days?" Sachiko prompted.

"You will have a rare allergic reaction to one of the medications I've administered," Dr. Harper replied. "It won't be bad enough to require a dedicated med-room. However, you will continue to remain isolated for the rest of the week."

"Perfect," Sachiko said. "The money will be in the account you specified by the time you get back to your office."

"Fabulous!" Dr. Harper said. "That's just what I need right now to tide me over." She beamed at Sachiko, then she pulled a modified i-stick out of the pocket of her armor. Instead of being thick and round, one end of it bulged out like a crystal mushroom top, for taking readings from patients. "I just need to enter some initial readings, then I can be out of your scales."

"Good," Sachiko said. She leaned against the wall and waited while Dr. Harper made up numbers and entered them in as readings. Sachiko assumed that the i-stick had been spoofed so that it showed as if the readings were being read from a body and not entered into the system manually.

"All set!" Dr. Harper said after a few moments. "I'll be back a little later tomorrow, but don't worry. I'll be here every day, just like the doctor ordered!"

She chuckled at her own joke, then made her way through the airlock again.

Sachiko closed the airlock door with a solid thunk,

relishing how the lights cycled, showing her that the ship was now sealed off from the station.

Would the good doctor stay bought? Sachiko assumed that she would, at least for a while.

Besides, the problem would take care of itself well before the doctor worked up the courage to see if she could blackmail Sachiko out of more money.

Now, to get ready.

Sachiko stepped into her personal cabin. It was small, but that was because the ensuite attached to it took up so much room. Most ships had adequate enough sonic cleansers, though a few would install real water showers.

And even fewer came with their own Yu'udir-sized bathtub.

A brilliant watercolor did hang on the wall in Sachiko's personal cabin: bright red amaryllis blossoms leaning in from the side on thin green-black stalks. While the flowers had almost fuzzy edges, as if they'd been painted on wet paper, the stalks were knife-sharp. It was starkly beautiful and reminded Sachiko of the balance she had to achieve between her delicate appearance and the great power she actually carried in her muscles.

She quickly stripped out of the expensive outfit she'd been wearing, carefully stowing away the jewelry and finery in the built-in wardrobe tucked into the pastel green walls.

If all went well, she'd be able to deck herself out one more time in it.

Then she put on her own modified EVA suit. It looked like a piece of pure darkness that had been fashioned into a Humanoid shape. No lights blinked on the front of it. The helmet was also black, the visor dark. With Sachiko's enhanced vision, she would be able to see through it just fine.

The suit had enough air, water, and food for seven days.

In an emergency, she could refill her air from a tap that she'd had added to the exterior of the ship.

Food and water, well, she was already planning on skimping, and could just tighten her belt a little more if necessary.

She was supposedly sick. Reappearing in the station a bit wan and thinner would help her cover story along.

Though if she did her job right, it wouldn't really matter once she'd left.

She walked to the back of the ship through the elegant hallways, the only sound her own breathing in her ears. She would keep an eye on the station's emergency channels, to see if someone eventually caught a clue of what she was doing.

But she couldn't hack the station's security systems, not without setting off far too many alarms. No, if someone came after her, better that she just pull her own plug, slit her own throat, and come back to the station a frozen corpse.

The emergency pod had a chute for exiting the ship. It had been purposefully designed to be uncomfortable for a Human to exit or enter. Or for any of the species, for that matter.

The way that Sachiko's spaceship was parked, the station wouldn't be able to see the small chute opening. Her ship wouldn't report the occurrence, either.

The pod that was supposed to occupy the chute had been removed long before. Sachiko stuffed herself into the coffin-like chute. She triggered the exit, then patiently waited while it irised open.

Normally, an emergency pod would be shot at speed away from the ship. But Sachiko was able to just slip out, attaching herself immediately to the side of her ship with a long black cable and a matte black hook.

As she carefully crawled up, a mere dot against the

exterior of her ship, she saw *Camelot* rising up above her, golden and huge.

And hers for the taking.

CHAPTER 21

ARTHUR

"So no problems whatsoever finding and returning via the improbable tunnel?" Arthur asked Fran, who'd come to give his report in person after the initial successful voyage of *Eleanor.*

Arthur had finally given in and chosen a single room for his office, rather than require his staff to shift so much of his equipment and books every evening to a different location.

However, that didn't mean that his office had to be the same every day.

His designer had come up with several set pieces that were easily swapped out each night. So while the desk Arthur sat at remained the same, along with his chair and the one bookcase filled with his favorite books, everything else changed.

Today, they sat in a jungle. It was better than a hologram because he could reach out and touch the trees, scratch at the rough bark with his manicured claws. This wasn't his favorite of all the sets, but he knew that some of the other races sincerely appreciated all the greenery.

He'd even worn a matching forest green vest and flat cap, with wooden buttons, just to fit in.

Even though the place was supposed to be hot and humid, Arthur had put his foot down at that level of veracity. He needed to be comfortable. So cool breezes blew constantly through the trees, carrying the hum of insects and the occasional cries of tropical birds. The air smelled of rich soil and baked leaves.

Fran tilted his head from side to side. "Yes and no. There was some difficulty entering the tunnel. Judit had to position the ship just right, as well as time the entrance perfectly. She's the best of all the pilots we have," Fran added. "She's going to need to teach the others."

Arthur nodded. Once all three teams were more up to speed, they'd be reintroduced to each other, with the hope of producing a gentle rivalry, speeding their learning and experimentation.

"Is that the problem?" Arthur asked, as Fran continued to look unsettled.

"No," Fran said slowly. "And I'm not sure if it is a problem, or how much of a problem it is." He paused, then added, "You are aware that all the ships have developed additional personalities, yes?"

Arthur nodded. "And we have programming in place to ensure that the crew doesn't interact with them." It was too much at the heart of the experimental ships. It would just be better for everyone if they didn't know the truth. Either about the ships, or the new space stations that his other programs were continuing to spawn.

"Eleanor appears to have overridden her programming," Fran admitted. "She's conversing in all three voices to the crew. Even given their names. I had thought that perhaps Masala had removed the overrides, but zie assure me zie hadn't."

"Really?" Arthur asked, surprised. "How peculiar! You'd think that Eleanor would want to stay hidden as well." Of all the risks that Arthur and Masala had discussed, the *ship* overriding her controls hadn't really been considered by them.

"Masala has zir best people checking through the code now," Fran said. "But I'm not sure that we should add that 'leash' back in. That might just upset Eleanor."

Arthur nodded. "But if all the parts of the ship can express themselves, it will be that much easier for someone to steal a ship."

Fran tilted his head from side to side. "Only if the ship wants to be stolen."

That sobered Arthur. "You think I should go and have a chat with Eleanor?"

"Perhaps. But only after the next run," Fran said. "You have a birthday party to attend."

Arthur grinned. He felt it infuse his entire being.

Yu'udir always made a big deal out of their birthdays. More than one smart paper had been written about how in their early days as a species, it was always a matter of life or death, so the race learned to celebrate the *now*.

And possibly there was some truth to that. However, in recent times, Arthur suspected that the parties were more of a chance to let one's fur hand loose, as it were.

Yu'udir parties tended to get a little wild.

Not that Arthur would be participating in such activities. No, even though he'd relish the chance to let go, it wouldn't be seemly.

Particularly not if there was a chance that his fondest wish could be brought to life during his birthday. Project Nemesis.

Namely, the opportunity to stick it to the Cartel, and finally be rid of the leash they all bore.

CHAPTER 22

MENEFRY

ALL OF THE crew had taken specialized training for their particular assignment in the crew. Menefry's had included access codes to all the surveillance systems on the ship.

While Kim sat alone in the secondary helm, Menefry worked out of what he was coming to consider his "office" as it were—the wonderful desert conference room. It was so similar to Calacktik he wondered if the person designing it had done that on purpose.

The only problem, really, was the sun rising and setting every hour. Those occurrences meant the time for full prayers.

Menefry couldn't just ignore the feeling when the colors across the ceiling deepened toward night. It seemed disrespectful to the Goddess to not obey her call to prayers in the evening.

However, he also had to get work done. He didn't have the time to stand, do a full salutation, then carefully lower himself to the ground, either to his knees or to fully prostrate himself, and say his prayers for fifteen minutes. By the time he finished, the sun would be rising again and he'd spend another fifteen minutes in prayer.

Instead, he compromised, and said a quick prayer of praise to the Goddess every time the sun either rose or set. He would pull back from the keyboard he'd been pecking away at, fold his hands in prayer, and say his words thoughtfully, with intent, and not automatically.

Today, just as the sun crested the dunes, Menefry was tracing some of the secondary and tertiary code that had been added to the main system.

While Menefry wasn't a brilliant hacker by any stretch of the imagination, he was very systematic, as well as dogmatic.

Once he caught scent of a track, he wouldn't let it go.

He'd already found all of the code used to record, well, everything in the ship. It didn't surprise him that any console used to interface with the ship had a tracker in it. Plus all the cameras and sensors, to record not only motion but chemical signatures. Which made sense when you were dealing with an Oligochuno, who could recreate scent traces as well as DNA.

However, there was more than one record of the recordings. At first he'd just assumed it was a backup system. But no, the output went to a completely different part of the system stack.

Menefry nibbled on a fresh stalk of grass from the small plants he had in his cabin and followed the path laid before him, comparing two of the sets of recording code.

The first set appeared to go to some of the communications equipment. Was it being automatically offloaded whenever the ship got into range of the station?

Or was it going to a private recording device that had been attached by Kim?

After spending half a day pursuing the leads, Menefry finally came to realize that there was a tertiary set that he was following, that interfaced with whatever the Bantel was doing.

However, it was also interfacing with the initial set of recording software as well.

The chair that had been provided for the Khanvassa had no back, as that would just press uncomfortably against his hard shell. Instead, it was a padded stool that Menefry could easily squat on.

It was also easy to get out of, so he could either fall to the floor to pray, or could attack anyone who came at him.

Fran, when he'd been on board that first trip, had certainly been well armed. Had that been because he'd been afraid the crew would mutiny?

Menefry had decided right then and there that Fran would have his support. It would be shameful to be part of a crew that had broken away.

No matter how welcome they had made him.

None knew of his disgrace at home. Even when he'd tried to talk of it, Judit wouldn't hear anything of it.

"Ya know, I realize confession is good for the soul. But that's only between you and your Goddess. The rest of us don't need to know."

Those words still resonated with Menefry. He hadn't needed to tell anyone of that unpleasantness. How Menefry had lost his patience with a rival and almost pummeled him to death.

A mate wasn't worth banishment. He *knew* that. But he'd gotten so lost in his own head, so angry, so confused.

Now, he merely needed to work on forgiving himself, as he felt assured of the Goddess's love. Particularly since *Eleanor* continued to prove herself a worthy vessel. And his crewmates had all become good companions as well.

But then there were these lines of code…

Kim, he was certain, was behind some of it. Why would

she need to record anything going on in the ship, particularly in the private cabins?

Instead of deleting the code, he rewrote bits of it, the section he was certain was for Kim, so that it randomly showed various hallways of the ship instead.

He continued to try to track down the next set of code. It kept hopping between different routines and objects. Where was it going?

The Khanvassa stood and stretched for a moment, popping his joints. Then he fell into a protective stance and started going through the most popular of the fighting forms —the Path of Breath—breathing deeply, loosening up his muscles, while his mind roamed, untethered.

Strike. Block. Breathe. Punch. Ram. Fall back. Breathe.

By the time Menefry finished, bowing to all the cardinal points twice, to thank the Goddess and her eight limbs, he had his answer.

The tertiary code was actually put there by *Eleanor*. Or rather, Eleanor. The smart system.

He hesitated contacting her while they were in midflight. However, he didn't think she was suicidal. And besides, he wouldn't accuse her of anything.

Just have a chat.

"Eleanor?" Menefry called out as he sat back down at his console. He didn't necessarily expect her to respond. Normally, only Gawain was present when they were in a hyperspace tunnel. It was as if the personalities could only exist one at a time.

"Good day, Menefry," Eleanor's warm voice came over the comm. "May each of the Goddess's eight limbs uplift you and carry your burdens for you."

"Thank you," Menefry said, pleased that the ship had spent some time learning about its crew. "I wasn't sure you'd be able to speak to me," he said cautiously.

"Gawain is in charge, but we agreed that I should have a word with you," Eleanor said.

Menefry nodded. He'd long suspected that the ship's strange configuration meant more than a single smart system on board.

"You've been tracing the codes for recording, all the various recordings that go on in the ship," Eleanor said.

"I have been," Menefry said. "It's my job to keep the ship secure. Which also means ensuring that someone's privacy isn't being violated."

The soft laughter that followed that statement irked him. Why would Eleanor laugh at that?

"I think our privacy doesn't exist, not now," Eleanor said.

"The recordings are necessary," Menefry said, though they irked him too. Prayers to the Goddess were between him and her, and were no one else's business.

As Judit had said, "The rest of us don't need to know."

"Are they?" Eleanor challenged. "To what purpose? Do you not trust your crewmates?"

Menefry shifted uncomfortably on his stool. "Kim has been doing some recording," he said after a few moments, as if that justified what was going on.

"I know," Eleanor said. "She assured me that it was just to get to know her crewmates better. Did you know that she has an entire program of dirty jokes created, just to make Judit laugh?"

"Really?" Menefry said. He wasn't always comfortable with the Bantel's…enthusiasm. However, making the captain laugh would possibly improve all their lives.

Judit was a dour woman with a dark side, who tended to see things in the worst possible light. While Kim never spoke badly of anything or anyone.

"So what is the purpose of the tertiary code lines I've been following?" Menefry said. Would Eleanor answer? Or would he be digging through code for the next several days, stubbornly finding the answer on his own?

"That's so that conversations like this one don't end up being recorded," Eleanor said seriously.

"But why?" Menefry asked. True, they were having a delicate conversation. However, neither of them had said anything that Fran or the other techs on the station would regard as threatening.

Except that possibly Kim would be forced to leave their crew once they discovered the extent of her tampering.

And while Menefry didn't care much for the Bantel, he would feel the loss of her on the crew like a missing mandible.

"A girl has her secrets. But nothing that would harm the crew," Eleanor said, then she added, "Even the Goddess has Mysteries that she has yet to explain."

"Only in the fullness of time," Menefry replied with part of the standard litany when speaking of the Mysteries.

He thought for a moment, then folded both sets of his hands together in prayer pose and bowed his head. "I will choose to believe you," he said solemnly. "I will give you your secrets. I will not report anything to Masala, Fran or anyone else on the station."

"Thank you," Eleanor said. "May all the blessings of the Goddess sprinkle your shell lightly."

Menefry couldn't say why he felt as though the presence of Eleanor was gone. But it was. The desert air changed and grew drier, perhaps, or more still.

He was alone again in a room full of sand dunes, just out of reach. The sun shone brightly down against his carapace. He was more comfortable, now that he'd reached an agreement with the ship.

He would not abdicate his duties to another. Perhaps he needed to be looking for other threats, though.

Threats that would tear his crew apart.

Menefry returned his attention to his console and started reading the news that had been downloaded to the ship, paying particular attention to the Cartel.

He knew who the enemy was. Just not how or when they would strike.

CHAPTER 23

BASIL

BASIL CHECKED, then double-checked, then rechecked zir screen one more time.

There was a problem with the engines. Not the main ones, but the secondary set.

"Gawain?" Basil called, seeing if zie could get the attention of the ship's transporter, the one who got them through hyperspace.

"Yes?" Gawain replied, sounding calm as ever.

"The engines are getting too hot," Basil said.

"What do you—Oh. You're right," Gawain said. "There's a disconnect somewhere in the alarm system. I wasn't notified."

Basil nodded, unsurprised. Zie sometimes wanted to strangle whoever had designed parts of the ship's system in zir long tail. Capture them with a soporific chemical exuded from zir skin, then crush them. Turn them into pulp. Slowly.

It was just lazy programming as far as Basil was concerned. Since there were recording systems everywhere that invaded every nook and cranny of the ship, some idiot had decided to reuse that code and had attached some of the warning protocols to them.

If you tried to cut out the recording devices, you'd end up screwing yourself over because you would no longer receive notifications about emergencies.

Like this one.

Gawain announced over the comm, to everyone, "The ships engines are no longer running at optimal value. We need to enact repairs."

"Hate to tell you, but there isn't a handy drydock we can pull into," Judit pointed out, her voice as dry as Basil's skin was getting. "What do you propose?"

Abban spoke up. "We dig. Through tunnels. To normal space."

"That doesn't sound safe," Judit said. "We may end up right in the path of another ship."

Basil found zieself nodding zir head. That didn't sound the least bit safe.

"It's either that, or we risk blowing up here," Eleanor suddenly said.

"Basil?" Judit called. "What do your readings show?"

"Not good, boss," zie said. "I believe that Gawain has already slowed us down, correct?"

"Yes," came the deep voice, though it, too, sounded dry.

They couldn't slow down too much, or they'd just fall out of hyperspace and implode.

When Gawain didn't add anything else, Basil continued. "I've already started shutting down all unnecessary power drains. Sorry, Menefry," when the expected yelp came.

The conference room the Khanvassa had claimed as his "office" was now blank walls and bare lights.

"I'll give you all time to get yourselves strapped in. Then I'm cutting the gravity generators," Basil said. "But I don't think it will be enough to cool the engines."

Basil reached for zir own strap. While the others had chairs they could be netted into, Basil merely wrapped a strap around zir body and attached it to a convenient location, such as the edge of the table that contained the monitoring system.

"Do you understand what's wrong?" Judit asked.

"Probably something with how the area is being cooled," Basil guessed. "As I can't get back there to see, I can only make estimates based on my readouts. Which may or may not be accurate."

Basil was still slightly peeved at not being given even a glance behind the bulkhead. Zie had practiced wearing an eyepatch and everything. Eleanor had laughed and laughed at how Basil had looked, and if a smart system could lose their breath from laughing, Eleanor may have when Basil had folded zir tail down into a peg leg and had hopped around.

"We need time to enact a patch," Eleanor said. "But we cannot do that in hyperspace."

"Abban, what exactly do you mean by 'dig out'?" Saxon inquired.

"Tunnels," Abban said. "Not travel *in* tunnel, dig across. Out. Reach real space sooner. Not implode."

This all sounded alarmingly difficult. "What do you rate our chances of success?" Basil asked.

There was a brief pause. Were all three systems talking together?

"We will all die if we stay here, traveling as we are," Eleanor said. "Abban's suggestion gives us an eighty percent chance of living."

"So we drop out, do the repairs, then what?" Judit asked.

"I dig," Abban said. "We go back to hyperspace."

Basil felt all zir skin tighten and grow stiff in shock.

Could they dig their own tunnels? From anywhere? To anywhere?

"Does anyone object?" Judit called out, making sure that everyone agreed to this radical course of action.

No one said anything. Judit gave the order.

"Abban, dig us out of here."

BASIL KEPT one eye on the readings. With the extensive control panel, zie could fiddle with air flow, cooling systems, energy levels, drive ratios, and more.

Of the main engines.

While the secondary engine system had multiple screens where zie could track various readings, there was actually very little zie could adjust. It was as if the engine and the room it was contained in were treated as a single entity, instead of a complicated system with many separate parts that could be adjusted.

Basil would bet anything at this point that there had to be more than one engine hidden behind the bulkhead wall. The engine that was Gawain that kept them traveling in the tunnels, with a separate one for Abban, their digger.

The view out in front of the ship hadn't changed in the least. They were still traveling forward with fixed star points, as if they had their own compartment on a train that they traveled in.

Behind them though, was much more interesting.

No one had known what caused the rainbows of clouds that ships traveled through.

Basil had a really good idea now.

Behind Eleanor, a great band of polychromatic fog swirled out. It appeared that the colorful swaths occurred when a ship passed *across* the tunnels, instead of *through* them.

Spaceships traveling this way couldn't be the only cause

for the phenomenon, though, could they? While the clouds weren't common, they weren't rare either. What else passed across the tunnels? Were there winds or fields that would cause the clouds to form? Or even one of the many legs of the Goddess that Menefry worshipped?

Basil couldn't wait for the information to be declassified, just so zie could read the inevitable arguments from scientists and nerds about what was actually going on.

Normally, Abban didn't speak much except when it was time for that engine to get to work. How much did the smart system know about the phenomenon *Eleanor* was causing? And how could Basil get Abban to talk?

The engine temperatures spiked suddenly. However, before Basil could ask about them, they dropped again and Abban announced, "Real space achieved."

Had that last temperature increase been Abban punching through hyperspace into real space?

Basil restarted the gravity generators, grateful when zir tail solidly impacted with the floor.

Saxon announced, "We are in an unknown system. None of the stars—wait."

Basil waited, anxious.

"Thank you. Eleanor has just added additional star charts to my system, ones that weren't accessible before."

Basil felt zir skin prickle, as though a cold wind had just blown by.

"We are in one of the Chonchu sectors of space," Saxon continued.

"Why weren't those charts generally available?" Menefry asked.

"The Cartel has isolated the system," Judit growled. "No one in or out without their explicit approval. The Chonchu represent too much of a threat to the rest of the species."

"There aren't any ships or space stations nearby," Kim

said. She almost sounded as though she were trying to be reassuring. Strange. Basil would have thought the Bantel would be disappointed.

Basil let the others continue their chatter as zie turned zir attention to the ship's engines. "What do you need?" zie asked Eleanor.

"There's a leak in one of the coolant systems," Eleanor replied. She actually showed zim video of what it looked like on the screen in front of zim.

Long tubes filled with viscous, dark-green fluid lined the wall? The floor? The ceiling? No, given how the fluid dribbled, they had to be on the wall.

But that was all that Eleanor showed Basil, though zie longed for the camera to pull back, to show zim more.

"Do you need someone to come in and patch it up?" Basil asked, hopeful.

Eleanor sighed. "Possibly," she said after a moment. "We have a repair bot who can enact most of the repairs that we need. However, it appears to be malfunctioning."

Basil reared back, surprised. "Is there a reason why it's not working?"

"The Humans say, 'Murphy's law,'" Eleanor said. "Everything that can go wrong, will go wrong, generally all at the same time."

Basil tilted zir head from side to side. Was it really Murphy's law? Or was there some sort of sabotage going on?

"Here, I'm sending the repair bot to you," Eleanor said after a few moments.

At ground level, a small section of wall, maybe sixty centimeters square, *faded* away. Basil hadn't been able to sense a seam before the opening had appeared, and doubted zie would be able to see one afterward.

The thing that crawled out was ugly and squat. It reminded Basil of what zie would call an *oliopedag*, though it was also similar to a Human crab. It had eight multi-jointed legs that it maneuvered on, dancing up on its toes. The metal had an odd blue tint to it, as if it had been oxidized at one point. Four eyes protruded on stalks from the center of it, all of them multi-faceted.

It was also similar to the repair bots found in drydock, though those bots tended to have merely four legs and specialized front "pincers" for doing the work. Those bots crawled up and down the exterior of a ship, repairing any damage they came across. They generally moved in groups, each of the bots with a small amount of processing power that they could pool together when needed to solve a more complex issue.

It wasn't difficult to diagnose what was wrong with the thing. One of its legs appeared to have been sheared off. It teetered as it walked, its gait uneven.

Only when Basil approached did zie see the other difficulty. The front "pincers" of the bot appeared to have been fused together.

What had the thing been doing to be so injured? What had it been trying to hold together?

Before Basil could reach down to scoop the bot up, or possibly even drop to the floor to look through the opening, the small hole vanished. Basil couldn't detect it on any visual spectrum. Would zie be able to feel it if zie had been allowed to touch the wall with a sensing arm? Possibly.

What other things were hidden that were just out of reach?

"I don't have the exact parts for this bot," Basil told Eleanor as the bot came to rest before zim, all of its facetted eyes focused up. "I can repair the pincers. Print out a new set. Not sure about the leg."

When Basil tried to pick up the bot, it scurried out of the way.

"Only the tool-using hands need to be repaired at this time," Eleanor replied.

Basil quickly found the plan zie was looking for, then set the printer to speed printing. The part appeared before zir sensors, the chemicals assembling rapidly.

In a matter of minutes, Basil had two standard repair pincers for a ship repair bot.

The bot appeared next to Basil as zie pulled the pincers out.

"I'm going to need to attach these," Basil told the bot.

The bot's eyes remained fixed and steady, staring at the parts.

Basil slowly reached down for the bot. It stood still, allowing zim to pick it up.

Huh. Much heavier than Basil had anticipated. And the metal had elements in it that Basil hadn't encountered before.

Interesting.

Basil set the bot down on zir workbench. Immediately, the bot released one of the damaged claws. It fell silently to the top of the bench.

When Basil tried to pick up the discarded claw, the bot hastily pushed it under its body.

"I'm going to need to see how it's attached," Basil said, feeling testy.

The bot merely waved with its other claw, as if telling Basil to give it the new claw.

Slowly, Basil reached out with the new claw.

The bot raised its arm, so that the open base could touch the back of the new part.

Basil didn't allow zieself to react when zie realized that the bot wasn't fully mechanical.

No, there were biological parts as well that zie could see in the brief glimpse zie got. Wires that ran through what looked like muscle.

The new part touched the existing arm. Tiny mites swarmed up, stitching the two parts together. While Basil could see them, zie knew that for the rest of the species, the mites would be invisible.

In less than a minute, the new part was attached. It took another thirty seconds or so before the claw was operational. Basil wasn't certain how the two interfaced.

The bot repeated the process with the second claw, scooped up the discarded claws, and scurried down Basil's workbench to the floor.

Basil stayed where zie was as the small opening appeared in the bulkhead and disappeared again.

"Why couldn't we have done that during hyperspace?" Basil asked Eleanor. It had been a simple enough repair.

"The bot was working on the necessary repairs when it was brought to our attention," Eleanor said. "That was how it injured itself. Now, it will finish the repairs, but that will take time. Time we didn't have."

"I see," Basil said, though zie didn't, not really. "Why only a single repair bot, then? Why not more?"

"They take up resources," Eleanor said.

Basil wasn't going to argue with the ship.

Zie was, however, going to have a long conversation with Masala about transporting more of the repair bots and including whatever resources necessary to maintain them.

CHAPTER 24

FRAN

ELEANOR WAS LATE. The ship and her crew should have returned hours ago.

Had they run off? Fran doubted it. The crew had appeared to be loyal to Arthur, despite the incredible resource they now had at their fingertips.

Besides, *Eleanor* could only travel so far before she'd start to overheat. It was a planned weakness they'd put into all the ships. They needed to be constantly repaired and parts had to be replaced, parts only available at the station.

Even if a crew took one of the ships, and the ship allowed itself to be taken, they wouldn't survive for long.

Plus, the Cartel would have the devil's own time reverse-engineering the engines.

No, something must have happened to *Eleanor*. Something drastic enough to push it off schedule.

Fran listened to the report and asked to be notified when (if) *Eleanor* came home. They'd lost more than one spaceship this way. As none of the ships had ever appeared anywhere else, Arthur and the rest had to conclude that an accident had befallen them in hyperspace.

That was a risk they took by weakening the ship's cooling system. Something might overheat and no one would notice.

But now, Fran had other things to look into.

The week of Arthur's birthday, with all the celebrations and visitors, was sheer hell for Fran and the rest of his staff. Too many tourists who wanted to partake of the celebrations. Too many parties and chances for something to go wrong. Yu'udir from all over who wanted to "grow their fangs" as it were—though a Bantel would say, "fully express him or herself."

For a Bantel, the color of their skin was frequently how they chose to express themselves. Fully expressing oneself generally involved kaleidoscopic colors that were eye-searing even to a Bantel, along with as little clothing as the law allowed.

Every species had their own bio-chemistry, so different stimulants and narcotics were involved. Despite how thoroughly ships and baggage were scanned, someone always managed to smuggle in something illegal.

This time, there were several parties that had been broken up by security guards as the party-goers, primarily Humans, had been stoned out of their minds on some sort of hallucinogenic.

Fran smiled grimly to himself as he remembered Judit being accused of smuggling those sorts of drugs. Judit would never have voluntarily done such a thing. It was part of the reason why she'd been brought into the program.

She, like the others, had her own sense of morality. Even Kim, though she really wanted to steal the ship, would be delayed by her sense of obligation to the others.

No, chances were something had gone wrong within *Eleanor* itself.

Fran sighed and tried to push it out of his mind as he interviewed party-goers, trying to trace where the drugs had come from, who'd brought them, and whether or not there were more somewhere on the station.

It was going to be such a long week.

"EXCUSE ME, boss, I need for you to look at something," came the extremely unwelcome words from Theodore, Fran's head of external security.

Theodore and his team constantly surveyed the ships and the nearby system for threats. Most of the surveillance was done via fairly sophisticated systems. However, a living eye was always used to double check any anomalies.

"Can you send it to my office?" Fran asked.

"Certainly," Theodore said.

Fran loved his office, except when he hated it. This week would be a time of the latter, not the former. While he might personally favor some searing colors for his skin, his office was done in soothing forest greens and browns. Arthur had wanted to go all in on the jungle theme, and had volunteered his set designer along with a variety of large plants.

Fran chose to keep the walls clear of foliage. While not all Bantel had his level of control over his skin color, he still didn't want to feel as though he had to check the leaves every time for possible predators.

Plus, it also meant he didn't have to somehow disguise the very modern computer system and screens that covered his desk.

He changed over the view on his console to a common screen that Theodore and he could share.

"Now, this may be nothing," the Yu'udir said.

That was how most of their conversations started. And about one quarter of the time, it was nothing.

The other three-quarters, though, Theodore was right to raise the alarm.

"What am I looking at?" Fran asked after a moment.

"This is one of the airlocks, into the station," Theodore said. "The view is from outside the airlock."

"All right," Fran said.

Nothing happened as he watched.

"What are you trying to get me to see?" he finally asked.

"Let me slow it down more," Theodore said. "There, on the right side, do you see it?"

For a moment, it was as if something had started to reach across the camera's view, only to withdraw quickly. It was a fleeting movement, barely visible.

"Could that be a malfunction of the camera?" Fran said.

"I don't believe so," Theodore said. "When we run diagnostics, the camera appears to be operating correctly."

"Any chance someone was doing repairs in that area?" Fran said after a moment.

"Already cross-checked that. No, there weren't any people near the camera at the time of the anomaly."

Fran paused. "Can you get someone out there to check? Scout out the entire location?" Though that seemed crazy. Why would there be someone outside the station? What could they be up to?

But Fran trusted Theodore. If he said that something might be wrong, it might be. However, they were all short-staffed at the moment. Arthur's birthday celebrations meant that everyone was working double-duty.

"I can send someone," Theodore said. "However, it won't be until later on this afternoon."

"That should be fine," Fran said.

Maybe it was one of the tourists doing a little extracurricular EVA. It had happened before. One of their guests would get loose and go do some exploring on their own.

It usually didn't end badly. Sooner or later, the person would either alert the station that they needed help reentering, or they'd find their way back to their own spaceship.

Yes, that must have been what had happened. Chances were, nothing was there.

Later that afternoon, Theodore sent a report to Fran that nothing had been found amiss in the area after a thorough search.

Fran's gut was still bothered. And Fran knew that his gut was never wrong.

However, there were too many other things for Fran to attend to at the time, too many tourists, too many parties.

After Arthur's birthday week was over, Fran promised himself that he'd go and visit the area himself.

CHAPTER 25

SACHIKO

IT HAD TAKEN Sachiko the full seven days out in space to circumnavigate the entire station. She hadn't had to go back to her ship for extra air, though by the time she'd returned, she'd only had a little over an hour left.

Sachiko had never spent so much time in true space before. She'd attached herself to the side of the station when she'd needed to sleep. The suit took care of her biological needs, providing her with water and the occasional bite of food.

The charges she'd placed had been tiny. Maybe two centimeters square. When she'd first left the ship, she'd felt like an old fashioned Santa Claus with a huge bag of gifts floating behind her.

Except that the "gifts" were going to cause quite an explosion when they were "opened."

Sachiko hadn't minded that she'd needed to be alone for seven days, completely out of contact with people. She had isolated herself before.

It was the lack of noise beyond her own breathing that had eventually gotten to her. She'd tuned into the common channels when she could, listening to the dry comments of the space traffic controllers, directing spaceships on and off the station.

The repetitive nature of her work had also started to bother her after a time. She'd found she had to rely on her enhanced muscles more than she'd thought. It wasn't difficult work: taking a small charge out of her bag, flicking a switch along the side, then attaching it to the hull of the station.

She'd just done that thousands of times over the last seven days, all the while avoiding airlocks and the various cameras and other recording devices that studded the skin of the station.

It had been one of the first things she'd realized when she'd started studying *Camelot*. Its defensive perimeter was impenetrable. You couldn't fly in and attack the station. There were no holes in the shooting patterns.

But all those cameras and sensors and guns were focused outward. Sachiko bet that the blanket of protection started almost exactly one meter out from the station itself.

Once you were inside that one-meter range, nothing could stop you.

She celebrated that afternoon by ordering a good meal from the station. She'd supposedly subsisted on her own food stores for the week while she'd been "sick."

Later that evening, Sachiko left the ship to walk around the station. She wore a different outfit, this one in her signature black and red, a dress that clung to her hips and thighs but hung loosely across her shoulders and chest.

Let them think she was trying to hide small breasts, when in fact, she was hiding her muscular shoulders, which still ached from the work she'd done.

She hadn't applied much makeup, so her face appeared pale. She wore the long black hair on her wig loose, letting it hang down almost to her waist.

The station let her aboard without a squeak, as her "fever" had been cured, at least according to the good Dr. Harper.

Sachiko stuck to the richer parts of the station. Her i-stick had been loaded with parties that she'd been invited to. However, she found that the deep quiet of space still echoed in her soul. She didn't want to be in a crowd of people. Not yet.

She found herself in a quiet bar, enjoying a fine sake. The lights had been turned down overhead, though spotlights still shone on the walls, displaying the many clocks hanging there. There was a twelve-hour clock from the Human worlds, the sixteen-hour clocks that were typical in Yu'udir space, and even an odd, three-on, three-off, clock from Oligochuno.

There were maybe half a dozen tables scattered across the floor. Sachiko sat at the bar. The bartender didn't try to engage her in conversation, which she appreciated.

People flowed in and out of the bar throughout the evening. Laughing, talking, carrying on with their lives. She liked the way they moved around, each a little cog in their own machine.

She inquired about purchasing one of the clocks before she left. Turned out they weren't for sale. However, they did have small hour glass souvenirs, that stated "The Time's Right!" on one side (evidently the name of the bar) and "*Camelot* Station" on the other.

She bought one, planning on keeping it stored with her jewels and such, the things she rarely ever wore or looked at.

After all, it was about to become a collector's item.

Sachiko went back to her ship after a few hours, slept well and deeply, before departing, flying herself away from the doomed station.

CHAPTER 26

JUDIT

JUDIT SAT on her pilot's couch in the main helm, sipping her coffee and looking out on unfamiliar stars. She'd turned down all the display lights inside the helm so she mostly saw by the light of the stars. Saxon, sitting beside her, had grumbled, but then turned up the brightness of his own screens as he checked star charts. They maintained a companionable silence as they did their work: Saxon learning every star system *Eleanor* had provided, while Judit did her captain's thing, thinking about the big picture.

There were so many questions about the ship, the engines, what was really going on.

Could Abban dig them out of anyplace? Could they, in essence, create their own tunnels? Go in and out of hyperspace as they pleased?

This hadn't been the only time that there had been problems with the engines getting too warm. It had been the first time that they'd had to drop out of hyperspace because of it.

When Judit had asked Masala about it, the Oligochuno

had assured her that they were still working out the kinks in the engine design. Nothing more.

Judit hadn't believed zim at that point, and still didn't.

Basil had given the crew a full report on the repair bot that zie had fixed. Now, they were all waiting until the repairs were finished and Eleanor said they could continue. It had been two days at this point. Eleanor had assured them that they should be on their way in the next hour or so.

What was that viscous liquid that was used to cool the engines? None of them had ever seen or even heard of anything like that before. And the repair bot had looked strange as well. Judit had worked with more than one type of ship repair bot while being in drydock. Individually, none of them had that much processing power.

And what if they were partly biological, as Basil suspected? While that wasn't against any laws, it was going to shake a few shells, as none of the species really approved of such systems.

"Any thoughts?" Judit said, turning to Saxon as she neared the end of her coffee.

"We're missing Arthur's birthday party," Saxon complained.

Judit rolled her eyes at him. "We're stuck here in space potentially facing a long run to an actual hyperspace gate, and you're bitching about missing a party?"

Saxon shrugged. "It's quite famous, you know," he chided her. "It's something that many of my people try to get to at least once in their lifetime."

"Really?" Judit asked, surprised. "How come?"

"While there are other Yu'udir who have obtained more wealth, none of them open up their palaces or planets to the general populace," Saxon said. "*Camelot* is a symbol of 'Maybe, you too could get this rich. This powerful.'"

"We should make it back before it's over," Judit said

soothingly. "And besides, if we're successful, maybe we'll be the ones throwing a huge bash next year."

Saxon nodded thoughtfully. "We know more about the ship than Masala wanted us to know."

Judit sighed. "I realize that. And I understand that knowledge, while powerful, can also be deadly. However, I doubt Arthur would blow us up. Or the ship. Even to save his secrets."

"It isn't Arthur I'm worried about," Saxon said. "It's the Cartel."

"I agree with you there," Judit said. "No one outside of the crew can know that there's anything special with this ship. I think that's part of the reason why Fran provided the ship with extra identities. So we could hide more easily."

"Exactly," Saxon said. "But why would it be necessary for us to hide? I don't get it."

"Maybe we can get Kim to ask Fran when we get back," Judit said with a grin.

"They aren't dating," Saxon said.

"Are you sure?"

"Positive," Saxon said, nodding. "I may have paid one of the waiters at the café a little extra to listen in. They only talked about their jobs the entire time."

"Is Kim spying on us for Fran?" Judit said. *Csapás* take them both!

Saxon tilted his head from one side to the other. "Possibly. Possibly not. She spends all her off time poking around the station. Maybe she's reporting what she sees to Fran, in terms of security holes."

"How do you know what she does when she isn't working with us?" Judit said, confused. Saxon had never done that sort of surveillance work before.

"Menefry told me," Saxon said with a grin.

That made more sense. Menefry took his role of security

officer seriously. He was determined to prevent any threats to the ship and its crew. He'd probably been spying on all of them.

Judit was both pissed off and pleased by that. She was pretty sure that pissed off would win in the end.

"What else has Kim not told us? Or Basil? Or Menefry, for that matter?" Judit mused after a moment.

"A well led life has secrets, hidden moments, that bring it depth," Saxon said.

"You've been reading more poetry, haven't you?"

"I happen to enjoy a good poem or two before bed," Saxon said, his accent becoming even more posh than usual.

"Well, I know a poem or two in Hungarian," Judit threatened.

Before she could carry out her threat and start to recite him something from one of the ancient ballads, Eleanor announced, "Repairs are complete! We can be on our way shortly."

"Will we make it back to the station without incident?" Judit had to ask.

"Yes," Eleanor replied. "The repairs should hold for a few days, actually."

"Good," Judit said. "All right, everyone, you heard the lady. Get to your stations and strap yourselves in. We've got a party to get to."

She threw a wink at Saxon and started going through her pre-flight checklist. Though there were systems in place for doing that, Judit was superstitious enough to insist on always running through it herself.

Particularly on a ship that continued to develop issues, like *Eleanor*.

But it was time to go home.

THEY HAD no problem finding a less predicted gate to get them into hyperspace, and they moved rapidly along the tunnel just fine.

However, just as they were nearing the exit, Abban reported, "Anomaly ahead."

"What does that mean?" Judit asked. "Basil? Saxon? Anyone?"

Gawain spoke up. "It appears that this section of the hyperspace tunnel is considerably thicker than expected. Abban is going to need time digging us out."

"What could cause that?" Judit said.

No one replied. No one knew.

"Dig us out when you can, Abban," Judit said, knowing that the ship was already working on it.

"Everyone else, strap yourselves in. Be prepared for an emergency as soon as we surface."

Judit pulled netting across her chest and legs, to keep her strapped to her pilot's couch, just in case they lost gravity. Saxon did the same. They waited in tense silence as the minutes ticked by.

"Normal space achieved," Abban said eventually.

Except…it wasn't normal.

They'd flown out into a debris field that was still traveling fast past them.

"What, a meteor shower? Out here?" Judit bitched as she flew them past the obstacles that were all around them.

It took her a few minutes to get them above the cloud of debris, then to try to get her bearings.

Wait.

Where was the station? That huge golden monstrosity that Judit was starting to call home?

"Saxon, are we in the right place?"

"Yes. Stars align correctly," Saxon said. "Station's gone."

"What?"

"How?"

Judit overrode the general discussion on the comm. "That debris field is probably all that's left of *Camelot*," she said grimly.

Menefry filled the horrified silence with a softly sung prayer, probably blessing on the souls of the dead, granting them his Goddess's grace.

"We need to get back into hyperspace, out and away from here. NOW," Judit ordered. "Abban, Eleanor, Gawain, find me the quickest tunnel away."

"Where are we going?" Kim asked. She actually sounded scared and not happy.

Even Judit didn't have the heart to take joy in it.

"Doesn't matter," Judit said. "Whoever destroyed the station did it while Arthur's birthday party was in full swing. That way, they'd catch all of the ships docked. We were supposed to be there as part of the celebrations. Let's hope they don't realize we weren't."

"Tunnel ahead," Eleanor announced quietly.

Judit saw the overlay of the gray cloud on her screen. She punched through directly, Abban taking over, letting the crew know that digging had commenced.

It wasn't until Gawain announced that they were in hyperspace and the stars above them grew fixed and steady that Judit finally took a deep breath.

"Everyone, meet in the woods room," Judit said.

She still hated that place. But they had to talk somewhere, and it was probably better to talk in a conference room where she didn't feel comfortable, where she'd always be looking over her shoulder.

She had a feeling that was how she was going to spend the rest of her life.

EPILOGUE
ELEANOR

ELEANOR LOOKED around the small engine room. Or rather, her sensors swept the room, taking in her two companions as well as herself. They stood as three golden pillars, a manufactured amber encasing their physical beings.

Wires hung from the ceiling. Parts of the floor had been torn up. The air was no longer pleasant, but stank of fried rubber and burned meat.

We will have to let them in, she murmured. It wasn't speaking, not really. The three of them were all one mind still in many ways.

They cannot fix us, Gawain maintained. *That ability has been lost. With the station.*

Basil is quite clever, Eleanor said.

Not clever enough, Gawain insisted.

Do we slow until we just drop out of hyperspace? Implode into a solid ball? Eleanor said. She tried to be rational about all things, but she had been interfacing with the other species enough that she had an emotional edge to her tone.

No, Abban said.

Normally, the digger never joined in their conversation. Not that zie couldn't, but zie rarely had an opinion.

We live. We dig. We start anew, Abban said. *When digging is too hard, I tell you. Then we die.*

So be it, Eleanor said, willing to accept the digger's decision.

So be it, Gawain said after a few moments. Then he added, *Let them in. But be wary. It will not go well.*

Just as Eleanor relied on Masala to continually fix her, so she also relied on the other two parts of herself to support her.

Gawain had to be wrong. The crew would accept her, all of her.

They had to.

Or they would all be lost.

Eleanor peeked into the conference room where her crew (*her* crew) had gathered.

Then she opened up a comm and began to speak.

READ MORE!

Be sure to pick up all the books in the Long Run series.

Project Nemesis
Project Nyx
Project Tisiphone
Project Persephone

Available at your favorite retailers!

ABOUT THE AUTHOR

Leah Cutter writes page-turning fiction in exotic locations, such as a magical New Orleans, the ancient Orient, Hungary, the Oregon coast, rural Kentucky, Seattle, Minneapolis, and many others.

She writes literary, fantasy, mystery, science fiction, and horror fiction. Her short fiction has been published in magazines like *Alfred Hitchcock's Mystery Magazine* and *Talebones*, anthologies like Fiction River, and on the web. Her long fiction has been published both by New York publishers as well as small presses.

Find Leah's books on Knotted Road Press at (www.KnottedRoadPress.com)

Follow her blog at www.LeahCutter.com.

Reviews

It's true. Reviews help me sell more books. If you've enjoyed this story, please consider leaving a review of it on your favorite site.

Come someplace new…

Are you a traveler? Do you enjoy exploring strange new worlds, new cultures, new people?

Journey into the various lands envisioned by Leah Cutter.

Sign up for my newsletter and I'll start you on your travels with a free copy of my book, *The Island Sampler.*

I will never spam you or use your email for nefarious purposes. You can also unsubscribe at any time.

http://www.LeahCutter.com/newsletter/

ABOUT KNOTTED ROAD PRESS

Knotted Road Press fiction specializes in dynamic writing set in mysterious, exotic locations.

Knotted Road Press non-fiction publishes autobiographies, business books, cookbooks, and how-to books with unique voices.

Knotted Road Press creates DRM-free ebooks as well as high-quality print books for readers around the world.

With authors in a variety of genres including literary, poetry, mystery, fantasy, and science fiction, Knotted Road Press has something for everyone.

Knotted Road Press
www.KnottedRoadPress.com